FROM THE ROCK STARS

A COLLECTION OF SHORT STORIES

FROM THE ROCK
STARS

EDITED BY ELLEN CURTIS & ERIN VANCE

ISBN: 978-1-989473-47-4

Distributed by:
Engen Books
www.engenbooks.com
submissions@engenbooks.com
First mass market paperback printing: April 2020
Cover Design: © 2020 Ellen Curtis

Engen Books thanks Ellen Curtis, Erin Vance, Matthew Daniels, Amanda
Labonté, and Matthew LeDrew for helping make this collection possible.

CONTENTS

Introduction
Matthew LeDrew

For years, Engen Books has produced an annual collection of the best genre fiction that Atlantic Canada has to offer: the From the Rock series. It has seen tremendous commercial and critical success and we couldn't have done that without two groups: our spectacular writers, and our amazing readers. We've been looking to find a way to thank both for years.

With COVID-19 in full swing and the world in isolation, we thought of no better time and way to show our thanks than to offer this collection of short fiction for free during the course of the crisis, and at no more than cost for the print book. Please enjoy these stories at no cost, and we hope that the worlds they bring you to is a brighter one.

From the Rock collections alternate between three main genres: Science-Fiction, Fantasy, and Chillers. This collection contains the best examples of all three, in roughly equal measure. All stories are kept to a PG-13 standard to be as widely accessible as possible.

Those who read the series regularly will notice that there are some names that show up again and again. These individuals are known as Rockers: authors who have been included in at least three different collections, and who have proven themselves excellent at each of the main three genres we've challenged them with. They are Ali House, Chantal Boudreau, Jeff Slade, Jon Dobbin, Matthew Daniels, Nicole Little, Paul Carberry, Peter J Foote, Sam Bauer, and, Shannon K Green. Collectively known as the best in genre fiction storytelling in Atlantic Canada.

Or, colloquially, as the Rock Stars.

Enjoy.

Matthew LeDrew
Engen Books founder

Nicole Little

Nicole Little is an award-winning short story author from St. John's, Newfoundland.

Her previous writing credits include 'Sweet Sixteen,' which won the June 2018 Kit Sora prize. She was featured heavily in both *Dystopia from the Rock* and *Flights from the Rock* in 2019, and in 2020's *Pulp Science-Fiction from the Rock*.

She has appeared in six anthologies from Australian publisher Black Hare Press, including *Eerie Christmas, Apocalypse, Storming Area 51, Monsters, Beyond,* and *Bad Romance.*

She is a mother of two.

She brings with her two stories from the fantasy genre: 'The Barrel of Fabrishemshire' and 'Imagine That.'

The Barrel of Fabrishemshire

The large oval-shaped metallic object that stood, half buried in the ground, in the middle of the town square had been there for as long as anyone in Fabrishemshire could remember. In fact, the square had actually been built *around* the object.

The townsfolk held a certain begrudging respect for it.

Most of them were afraid not to.

Lysander Drake, aged 8 and a half, was a precocious child. On days when her mother went to the farmer's market Lysander requested she'd be left in the gardens of the square. She liked to observe the bumble bees as they buzzed amongst the flowers and all the busy people who walked past. Or so she insisted.

In reality she wanted to watch The Barrel.

It had *always* been called The Barrel but not officially so until 1961 when Walter Peabody, having tended the gardens all through his teens, placed a hand painted sign at the foot of the object:

`The Barrel of Fabrishemshire. DO NOT TOUCH.`

And there it still remained, faded but readable. Walter was now just a few short months' shy of retirement.

On this particular day, the 18th of July, the sun was high and bright in the sky. Amelia Drake wheeled her young daughter along the cobbled path, placed a kiss upon her flaxen head and locked the wheels of her chair next to a Bougainvillea. She paused for a moment. She was hesitant to leave the girl alone here but Lys would hear tell of nothing else.

"I'll be back soon my dear."

"Ok Mummy! Goodbye!"

With a slight, bemused shake of her head, Amelia set off at a steady pace for Athlone Place where the market was held each weekend.

Lysander listened to the receding footsteps of her mother. When the sound had faded, she glanced over her shoulder to be sure, and then unlocked the brakes on her wheelchair, pushing herself closer to The Barrel.

It towered over young Lysander. With a curious eye she took in its smooth polished surface, how it somehow absorbed rather than reflected the midday sun. It emitted a mild low-frequency hum that everyone else seemed unaffected by. Lysander felt it though. It thrummed along her veins. And the closer she was to it, the stronger the drone became.

It was not an unpleasant feeling.

"Hello?" she whispered, glancing around to confirm that she was, indeed, alone. She felt a bit foolish but it had taken her ages to work up the nerve. "Is … is anyone there?"

Lysander wheeled herself closer still to The Barrel; she was now flush with the base. No weeds or grass came even close to touching it. Clearly, Mr. Peabody took his job very seriously. Taking a deep breath, she stretched out her fingers. Mature beyond her years, she would have denied her fear at that very moment, but her tiny hand trembled all the same.

It was warm and smooth. Her fingers tingled.

THEY WILL COME. TIME GROWS SHORT. YOU MUST PREPARE.

She gasped and her hand dropped to her lap.

"Who said that?!" she demanded, though she knew the voice had spoken only in her head.

"Who said what?" came a gruff voice from behind her. "You shouldn't be that close to it you know!"

Walter Peabody shuffled slowly up beside her. Lysander swallowed nervously, expecting to be in trouble: Mr. Peabody was notoriously protective of The Barrel.

"Sorry sir. I ..."

"Did you touch The Barrel?"

She nodded reluctantly, chagrined.

He sighed. "Did it talk to you? Tell me the truth now!"

Lysander's eyes widened. All she could do was nod.

Walter scratched his grizzled chin. *"The child will lead the way."* He said as he regarded her through narrowed eyes. "That's what it told me back in '61 when I touched it myself. 'Spose that's you. Been waitin'."

Lysander stared, opened mouthed.

"Quit yer gaping girl. See what else it has to say."

And so, hand placed firmly on the surface of The Barrel, Lysander relayed a long list of instructions to Walter. He dutifully and neatly transcribed them into a small notebook he kept in the front pocket of his shirt. By the time Amelia Drake returned to the square, punnet of strawberries in hand, Walter was long gone; a sense of urgency in his step. He had much to do over the next few days.

Back at home, Lysander pondered how to explain everything to her mother. She wheeled herself into the kitch-en where Amelia was preparing a salad for dinner.

"Mummy ... we need to talk."

A pregnant summer moon hung low and heavy in the early morning sky as a ragtag assortment of charac-ters made their way to the center of town. Dawn was still several hours away. They came to a stop in the square, gathering around The Barrel. There were not as many as Lysander had hoped – her mother, Mr. Peabody, the Sher-man's and their young twins; Dr. Aiden Folpp; Brenda Okpik and Clary Freemont, both nurses; Farmer Ted and a few others who had been convinced by the earnestness of Lysander and Walter's story. There were just twenty-two of them.

It was time. Lysander and Walter approached The Bar-rel, looked at each other and nodded. Simultaneously they placed their hands on the sleek, silver surface. Almost at once a strange faint whirring sound reached their ears; the object emitted a warm ethereal glow that soon enveloped its custodians. Amelia Drake gasped and, though her hand reached out for her daughter, she did not touch her.

Then, abruptly, it stopped.

Lysander and Walter smiled and turned to face the small gathering.

"It's ready."

Behind them, a low rumble arose and the ground quaked beneath their feet. Wary but consumed with curi-osity, they craned their necks for a glimpse of what might happen next. The children clung to their parent's legs and watched on in wide-eyed wonder as an opening appeared in The Barrel. A door. A small ramp slid forward; Walter looked to Lysander for permission and once granted, he placed his hands on the handles of her chair and began to push her up the ramp.

"Follow us!" she called, her face radiant with joy.

Amelia trailed her daughter up the ramp, the others behind her in succession, stepping into the darkness beyond... and what would be their salvation.

A day passed. And then a week. An entire year, almost to the day had passed, when things upon the surface finally went awry.

In those twelve months' prior, the townspeople had patted themselves on the back for not falling for the lies of Lysander Drake and Walter Peabody. Nothing had happened. A complete fabrication. They called them false prophets and other things that could not be repeated in polite company.

When the morning of July 20th rolled around, it was expected to be an ordinary day like any other.

Until it wasn't.

The first blast hit a hillside on the outskirts of town around 9am. Farmer Ted's homestead and pasture, abandoned the year before, was completely obliterated. A large smoking crater took its place. It sent the residents into a full fledged panic.

At 9:13 am an explosion rocked the east side of town. What wasn't immediately cremated, erupted in flames. As ashes fell from the sky like snow, people could be seen fleeing towards the town square. They pounded upon the surface of The Barrel, begging and screaming until they were hoarse.

What followed was a series of well orchestrated strikes

that left Fabrishermshire smoldering in ruins.

When the noise had settled, The Barrel could be heard emitting a series of sharp beeps – if there had been anyone left there to hear it that is. Smoothly, it descended into the ground. A small dimple in the dirt the only record that anything had ever been there.

When the first alien ship landed and its inhabitants set foot upon the Earth, they appeared quite pleased with their achievements. No one would have understood the language that they spoke but if they had, they would have learned that there'd been no real purpose behind the destruction. They had done it simply because they could. They collected a few human bones as a souvenir but otherwise, they didn't stay for very long. There was more fun to be had elsewhere on this planet.

Perhaps one day, when the lands are once again habitable, The Barrel will rise and a new town square will rise around it.

After all, history does have a way of repeating itself.

Imagine That

When she was a little girl, she had a fairy door in her room. She left childish offerings of friendship at the entrance: shells, buttons, shiny bits and bobs. But then, much to her mother's regret, that little girl got older and found she had no need for silly stories or foolish games. She grew up; she moved away, and like everything else, it was pushed to the back of her mind - a faded but pleasant childhood memory.

Life has gotten the better of her lately and she is so tired. For the first time in over a decade, she has returned home for a visit. Tonight she finds herself ensconced in her old bedroom, cozy beneath the pink coverlet of her bygone years, thinking back on the follies of her youth. She is adrift somewhere in the divide between wakefulness and sleep ... and that's when she hears the noise. A slow knock, knock, knock.

It's coming from the closet.

A long forgotten wisp of memory floats to the surface as her feet tread softly across the chilled floor. She is not surprised by what she finds when she pushes aside the hanging clothes, perhaps part of her had known it was there all along; calling her back. She brushes her hand along the roughly hewn surface of the door as the faint strains of lively music drifts from within. She pulls lightly on the sculpted handle and hopes that maybe this time, they will let her stay.

Ali House

A native Newfoundlander, Alison is a graduate of the Fine Arts program at Sir Wilfred Grenfell College (MUN), and past recipient of the Golden Crescent Wrench Award. Her short story, 'The Price of Beauty' won the December 2018 Kit Sora Award.

Her first novel, *The Six Elemental*, was released in October 2016. Its sequel, *The Fifth Queen*, was published in March 2019.

She is the only person to have short fiction published in all of Engen's open-call short story compilations, including *Sci-Fi from the Rock, Fantasy from the Rock, Chillers from the Rock, Dystopia from the Rock, Flights from the Rock, Pulp Science-Fiction from the Rock, Bluenose Paradox*, and *Kit Sora: The Artobiography*.

She currently resides in Halifax, Nova Scotia, where she works in arts administration and spends more time than a person should in and around theaters.

The first collection of her short fiction, *The Lightbulb Forest*, was released in February 2020.

She brings with her her new fantasy story, 'A Fairy Tale,' and her science-fiction story 'Authentic New Island Experience™,' reprinted from *Dystopia from the Rock*.

A Fairy Tale

Once upon a time there lived a princess. She had an older brother, who was a prince, and a mother and a father, who were the King and Queen of a very nice land.

This princess grew up learning the ways of a Queen. She was taught to be nice and polite, and to never speak too loudly or too much. She was instructed to be kind and fair to everyone in the land, and to put other people's interests ahead of her own. She wore beautiful gowns made of the finest silks and spent most of her time sitting quietly and listening to other people talk.

The day before the princess' sixteenth birthday her mother called her in for a talk. Her mother explained that it would soon be time for her to marry a prince and move to another kingdom where she would eventually become a Queen. The princess did not want to leave her home or her family, but she understood that all princesses had to marry princes so that they could become Queens and help their King rule the land.

Then her mother explained exactly how she was to be married. She could not just meet a prince and fall in love – oh no – the prince had to prove his worth. The princess would be taken from her kingdom and placed in a castle, where she would live in the highest room in the highest tower, and there she would wait for her prince to come. Her only company would be a few servants, who would cook and clean for her, but were not allowed to socialize with her.

From all over the land princes would come to this castle to rescue her and win her hand. Many would fail, but one day a prince who was worthy of her love would surpass every obstacles and save her. Then they would kiss and fall in love and be married and live happily ever after. That was how a princess found a prince.

So on the day of her sixteenth birthday, the princess left her home and family and all the people she had learned to serve, and traveled to such a castle. Her carriage passed through a haunted wood, over a precarious rope bridge, past a pack of angry dogs, and through a wall of prickly vines. After the vines was the final task – a fire-breathing dragon. She was not worried as she traveled because she knew that nothing would harm her. She was a princess, after all.

And so, in the highest room of the highest tower, she waited. The room contained all kinds of comforts, and many materials for her to continue her embroidery. It also contained a magical glass that would show her the progress of the princes who tried to rescue her. A few days after her arrival she watched in the glass as a prince made his way through the haunted wood without being terrified only to turn back after nearly falling off the rope bridge. She was disappointed but assured herself that he was not her true love. A short time later another prince came but he turned back without even making it through the haunted wood.

Over the next couple of weeks she watched as many princes tried and failed. There was one who made it all the way to the dragon, but was unable to defeat the fierce creature and had to leave with a broken sword and scorched armour. Despite these failures the princess refused to be disappointed. Someday her prince would come and rescue her.

As time passed, she began to play a game where she would look at the prince and try to guess where he would fail in his task. If he looked unsteady on his horse then he would likely turn back at the rope bridge; if he was impeccably dressed then he would have trouble with the sharp, twisted vines; if he hesitated before entering the haunted woods then he would not get far at all. This game, like all games, was fun at first but became less fun the more she played it.

Days turned into weeks, which turned into months, and still she was not rescued. She began to grow restless. Nobody had told her how long she would have to wait. How long would it take for her prince to arrive?

At first she'd maintained a careful distance from the servants, as her mother had instructed, but as time passed she began to crave human interaction and tried to initiate conversation. Unfortunately the servants refused to talk with her and kept their space.

The rules stated that she was not allowed to leave the castle until she was rescued, but there was nothing that said she had to stay in her room the entire time. She knew it was expected of her to remain in her room, waiting patiently, but as time passed she knew she needed something other than embroidery to keep her sane. At first she was afraid to leave – for what would happen if a prince made it through the obstacles and she was not there? – but then she realized that she could take the glass with her, and if she saw a prince make it past the dragon she could hurry back to her room to wait for him.

During her exploration, she uncovered rooms full of treasures – swords, textiles, coins, and jewelry. She brought some of the textiles to her room and began sewing them into dresses – staying within the accepted fashion at first, but later experimenting with different styles. She wondered if the styles of the kingdom had changed or if they were still the same. She wondered what her parents were doing and if her brother had rescued a princess of his own. She wondered if they were thinking of her.

When the textiles began to bore her she picked out a small sword from one of the rooms and practiced swinging it around. She had watched many princes wielding swords in their attempts to rescue her, and she tried to imitate them. Although she was clumsy and tired easily in the beginning, soon her arms grew stronger and she was able to swing a heavier sword with ease and grace.

Then one day she noticed that the princes were becoming fewer and fewer. At first there would be a prince almost every day, but now weeks would pass in between attempts. She wondered what would happen if they stopped coming. There were stories of princesses who had to wait hundreds of years for their prince to come, but they were always asleep and their youth magically preserved. Would she grow old in here? There were no stories of older princesses being rescued, only the beautiful and young. If no prince was able to rescue her, would she have to live out the rest of her life in this castle, alone? How many princesses went un-rescued?

The day after her seventeenth birthday she decided that enough was enough. She was not going to waste the rest of her life waiting for someone else to rescue her.

First, she used some of the plainer and tougher textiles

to make traveling clothes. The she sewed herself a knapsack, which she could keep extra clothing and coins in. She also packed some gems and small golden objects that might come in handy on her journey if she ran out of coins or if someone refused to take her currency.

When she was ready, she awoke early and dressed in trousers, a tunic, and buckled a sword around her waist. It felt strange to wear trousers, but she knew that they would be more practical to travel in. After slinging her knapsack on her back, she put on a small cape with a hood, to protect against the elements, and headed down the tower.

Finally, she stood in front of the castle doors. Taking in a deep breath, she opened them.

The sunlight that had come in through her single window was nothing compared to the beams that radiated from the sky. She stood there for minutes, feeling the warmth on her skin – skin that had not seen the sun for a year. It was then that she knew she had made the right choice.

The dragon was easy enough to get past. It always slept during the early morning, so she simply tip-toed past it. The vines were covered in sharp thorns, but she used her sword to chop through them – using a method she had seen a few princes employ, which was to slice each individual branch instead of just stabbing any-which-way.

The dogs were easily distracted by the meat that she had taken with her and paid her little attention as they ate. She hesitated before the rope bridge, which was swinging wildly across a great chasm, but refused to stop. She took it slowly and carefully, feeling a great sense of relief when she finally made it to the other side. After that it was only the haunted wood left. The ghosts and voices did not scare her as she had seen and heard them many times in her glass. Instead of listening to them, she concentrated on the sound of the leaves crunching under her feet, and the sight of the sunlight streaming through the leaves, feeling more alive than she had in her entire life.

Outside the forest she stopped, unsure of what to do next. To the West was her former home, but she did not want to travel there. Her mother would never forgive her for leaving the castle and would send her back straight away.

No, she would travel East instead and visit far off lands. She would explore the world and meet many different people, eating and drinking and telling tales. And she would make up her own rules for how a person should live his or her life.

As she walked she came upon a handsome prince traveling on a white horse. He seemed unsteady in the saddle, as if he was not yet accustomed to riding, but his face was determined.

"Hello young lad," he said to her, mistaking who she was because of her strange attire. "Are these the haunted forests?"

"Yes," she replied.

"I have heard that there is a beautiful princess who is trapped in a castle not far from here. The haunted forest is but one step towards her."

"That it is."

"I am going to rescue her and then we will marry and live happily ever after."

She looked at him carefully. It was doubtful that he would make it past the rope bridge with his lack of balance, let alone be able to face a fire-breathing dragon.

"Wouldn't you rather travel to a nearby village and have a nice meal?" she asked. "Maybe you will meet a beautiful maiden there."

The prince scoffed and held his chin held high. "I could never. I am a prince, and a prince must rescue a princess and marry her and then become King."

"You could do things differently," she suggested.

He shook his head. "This is the way that it is done and the way that it will always be done."

She sighed. "Then I wish you good luck on your journey."

The prince bowed his head in thanks and rode off towards the forest.

Once he was gone, the princess turned to the East and smiled.

Authentic New Island Experience™

Looking for an exciting place to travel? Why not visit New Island Ltd.! Formerly known as Newfoundland, trust us when we say the only thing that's changed is the name! Experience our stunning vistas and breath-taking views, while enjoying the Authentic New Island Personalities™ that the island is known for. Wander through one of our many small towns and admire the natural scenery while getting to know the local characters. Or, if you're looking for a more modern experience, visit the bustling city of New St. John's where you can grab a pint with a pal and dine on the finest local delicacies!

Worried about your daily consumer allowance while on the island? Don't be! Purchase a Local Traveller's Pass to cover all your basic needs or get more bang for your buck with a High Roller's Pass. Or upgrade to an Unlimited Pass and consume as much as you desire! Whatever your needs are, we have a Pass for you!

See majestic ocean creatures on a whale watching boat ride or travel north on an iceberg tour! Hike the magnificent mountains of Gros Morne Park or discover the magic of Lanse Aux Meadows! Get 'Screeched In' and eat as much Jigg's Dinner as you can handle! New Island Ltd. has it all!

There was a brief moment of silence as the commercial ended, the jingling tune fading into nothingness as the logo for New Island Ltd. appeared on the screen. The logo remained for a few seconds before changing into an image of rolling waves beneath a cliff. The jingle started up again and the commercial repeated itself for the seventh time.

As much as Dana hated the commercial, she couldn't handle the silence of the apartment. She needed some kind of sound in the background, and this was the only channel that didn't cost any money to watch.

If Jocelyn had been here, she would have told Dana to turn the television off before that jingle drove her insane. She also would have told her to stop crying so much. All those tears would surely dehydrate her, and she'd run the risk of going over her daily water allowance.

But that was the problem. That was why Dana couldn't stop crying.

Jocelyn wasn't here.

©

"How ya' gettin' on?"

Dana snapped back into reality. The lush green forest she'd been dreaming of was replaced by the hard, plastic truth of the Valley Mall food court she was currently sitting in. Grass, leaves, and sunshine quickly transformed into Some Nice™ restaurants and Best Sort™ shops that populated malls all across the island.

Turning to her right, Dana looked up at the smiling brunette whose cheerful voice had shattered her daydream.

"Are you Jocelyn?" she asked.

The brunette nodded. "Sorry I'm late. There was a hell o'va line up at Timmy's. Should'a known better than th' think there wouldn't be a line up at th' mall." She took a sip from the cup in her hand and sat down across from Dana. "So, yer lookin' for a roomie?"

Nodding slowly, Dana wondered what she'd gotten herself in to. When they'd spoken over the phone to set up the meeting, Jocelyn hadn't sounded so... small town.

"And you're looking to move out of the boarding house?" Dana asked, trying to keep her voice pleasant.

Jocelyn smiled. "Yup. Gotta feel some freedom under me wings. Them women running th' boardin' houses got eyes like hawks. Can barely take a breath without one of 'em knowin'."

Dana tried to return the smile, but she knew it must look forced. "And the price of rent won't be a problem?"

She nodded again. "I gotta job at th' Some Nice™ Bakery on West Street, sos I can afford th' rent. I assumes all th' taxes are included? Water, electricity, police, fire, whatnot?"

"They are. We get a bit of a break, because there are two apartments in the house, so we share the city maintenance and local maintenance taxes with the other tenants. Also, the landlord's an old family friend who babysat me when I was younger, so he was able to give me the family rate instead of the unmarried woman's rate."

"Ah, that's why th' rent's so affordable," she smirked. "Heck, I'd let someone babysit me now if it'd get me a deal like tha' one."

Dana couldn't help laughing. It seemed that Jocelyn had a sense of humour, which was encouraging. "Would you like to see the apartment?" she asked. "It's only one block away."

Jocelyn's eyes widened. "You lives near th' mall? Whatta grand deal. I'd love ta see th' place."

Dana stood up and gestured for Jocelyn to follow her.

She barely said anything during the walk, as Jocelyn didn't stop talking about what it had been like to move from Rocky Harbour to Corner Brook. Every word was pleasant and absolutely dripping with her North-coast accent. Dana wondered if the accent would lessen after a few years of living here or if it'd stay that way forever. As much as she didn't want to give up her apartment and move into one of those boarding houses, she wasn't sure if she could handle listening to that every single day.

They quickly reached the apartment, which was on the second floor of a former two-story house. "So, what'd happened ta your old roomie?" Jocelyn asked as they made their way through the apartment. "Oh, sorry," she said, stopping in her tracks. She paused and took a moment to compose herself. "So, what happened to the person you were living with? Why did she move out?"

It took Dana a few seconds to comprehend what had just been said. The un-accented words sounded as if they should be coming from someone else's mouth, but there was nobody else around.

Jocelyn laughed. "Sorry about that. You know what it's like growing up in a Designated Small Town. All accent, all the time. It's a hard habit to shake."

"Wow." Dana was truly taken aback. "You sound so normal now. Not that – I mean – it's just that... Oh, god..." She put her head in her hands. She needed to stop talking.

"It's okay," Jocelyn said, her voice light and cheerful. "After eighteen years in a DST, it's hard not to put the accent on whenever I'm in public. I always get paranoid that tourists might be within earshot, and I've made it this many years without getting fined for 'ruining the illusion'." She dramatically rolled her eyes.

Dana laughed, feeling the tension melting away. "Sorry. I grew up in Corner Brook, so I've never had to deal with laws that strict. I can't imagine what it's like."

"Honestly, it's like anything else – you get used to it. But it's refreshing to live somewhere that you can relax. Performing 24/7 is *exhausting*." Jocelyn sat down on the couch. "But I was asking about your previous roommate. Do you mind talking about her?"

She shook her head. "Erin... Erin had been friends with me since junior high. When we moved in here, we knew that it was only a matter of time before her boyfriend proposed and she'd get married and they'd get a house to live in. Sure enough, a few months later, he did, and they started wedding planning. Then, a few weeks ago, about two months before the wedding, his relatives in Nova Scotia contacted him, saying that they were willing to sponsor his move off the island. The only problem was that they couldn't afford to sponsor two people. He didn't want this opportunity to pass him by, so he called off the wedding, did up the paperwork, and moved away. After that, Erin married the first decent guy she came across and moved out. They've got a house up on Glenhaven Boulevard."

Jocelyn let out a slow breath. "Wow. That sucks."

"Yeah. Makes me never want to get my hopes up. About anything."

"Well, if it helps my application, I don't plan on getting married any time soon." Jocelyn smiled.

Dana returned the smile. "It definitely tips the scales in your favour."

©

Jocelyn moved in a few days later and the two of them

quickly grew close. At first Dana found the way that Jocelyn unconsciously slipped into her old accent a bit much, but she knew that it wasn't done on purpose. Jocelyn was a genuinely nice person, and Dana was glad to have met her – even with all of her Designated Small Town tendencies.

"You've got to play the game," Jocelyn said, tapping Dana playfully on the nose.

Dana frowned and waved Jocelyn's hand away. She'd come home from her date early, having decided that enough was enough two hours in. She'd been hoping her roommate would offer commiseration, but apparently that wasn't to be the case.

"I don't want to," Dana complained, walking over to the couch and falling onto it dramatically. "Dating is stupid."

"It won't kill you," Jocelyn replied, crossing her arms. "You know, you always have to make things more difficult than they actually are."

Dana frowned again. She wasn't the person who'd thought of mandatory dating for all citizens, or the person who'd included it in Govern-Corp's Tourism Laws, so how was she the difficult one? It wasn't her fault that the guy she'd gone out with tonight had been utterly wrong for her, so why should she be punished for not wanting to go out with him again?

Jocelyn sat down next to her. "The Rom-Cops will be easier on you if you look like you're making an effort. You don't have to get married, just date him for a few months before making up an excuse to dump him, and then move on to the next guy."

"But it's so stupid..."

"You know that if you don't go on a date at least once

a week, you'll be fined. And you've already got two fines on your record. A few more of those and they'll get suspicious and investigate you, which wouldn't be good for either of us." Jocelyn gave her a knowing a look. "Do you want to end up in a detention centre for the rest of your life – or worse – all because you didn't want to go on a few stupid dates?"

Dana sighed. "I know, I know. I'm just tired of it all."

"Well, grab a cup of Some Nice™ coffee, get your second wind, and suck it up."

She gave Jocelyn an unimpressed look. "I cannot believe you just said that."

Jocelyn smirked. "You can take the girl out of the DST, but you can't take the DST out of the girl."

It would be wise to take Jocelyn's advice, and Dana knew it. Jocelyn knew how to look like she was following the government's rules while secretly maintaining her own agenda. Her pleasant attitude and friendliness with tourists had been noted by Govern-Corp, and whenever she'd 'accidentally' stepped out of line, they'd been much more lenient with her than they would with any other citizen.

Citizens living in DSTs were paid to act like charming locals for the tourists, and with the high cost of living on New Island Ltd., not many of them could afford not to. Living in a DST meant being constantly aware of the Quality Control Agents who patrolled the whole island, writing up anyone who was caught out of character or causing trouble for Govern-Corp.

It sounded like the worst kind of life to Dana, who'd surely be in a detention centre by now if she'd been unlucky enough to be born in a DST. Corner Brook was the perfect size for her – too big to be a quaint small town, but too small to be as bustling as the capital city. They still had to be friendly and nice to all the tourists, but not at the same level as those in DSTs.

"But he talked through the entire movie," Dana groaned, unable to let the subject drop. "It's been so long since I've been to one, and he had to ruin it with his incessant chatter."

Jocelyn laughed. "You could have simply avoided the movies next time."

"Ugh. When you say things like that it sounds so... rational." She sat up and put her head on Dana's shoulder. "I just wish that I could date who I wanted."

"The mandate of Govern-Corp is to promote the prosperity of New Island Ltd. and all its citizens through a rich tourism trade, which includes creating a safe, non-political environment where tourists from all over the world will not feel uncomfortable." When Jocelyn finished quoting policy, she kissed Dana on top of her head. "At least they can't govern us inside our home."

A smile appeared on Dana's face. "Yeah. At least we have that."

Outside these walls they could never be anything more than friends, but in here nobody could tell them that what they felt was wrong.

"Have you ever wondered what it would be like to live normally?" Jocelyn asked softly. "Before Govern-Corp purchased this island and the Tourism Laws were passed?"

"All the time," Dana replied honestly.

"What if it were possible? What if we could?"

She straightened up. "What are you talking about?"

Jocelyn leaned in close and her voice went low. "Vineland."

Dana was confused. "You mean, what the Vikings called this island back in 1000 AD? Are you talking about the Viking settlement at Lanse Aux Meadows? That's even more tourist-themed than Rocky Harbour."

"No," Jocelyn shook her head. "The new Vineland. Surely you've heard the rumours. No Tourism Laws, no taxes or fines... It's the promised land."

It sounded vaguely familiar to Dana, but in a fairy-tale kind of way. Vineland was a fantasy for adults, a long-abandoned settlement that had been reclaimed by people sick of living under Govern-Corp's rules. It was supposed to be like the good old days, before Canada sold the island and all its resources to Govern-Corp for a tidy sum, and it was most likely a complete and total fiction.

Anyone who talked openly about going there was never heard from again. Some dreamed that those people had actually made it to Vineland, but Dana wasn't so optimistic. They had most likely 'disappeared', like the majority of the island's unhappy locals. Troublemakers didn't last long on New Island Ltd.

"Vineland's a fantasy," she replied. "It doesn't exist."

Jocelyn gave her shoulder a squeeze. "Ah, there's that pessimism I love so much."

"If it existed, I'm sure Govern-Corp would quash it. They'd destroy something like that twenty times over."

"But," Jocelyn was getting excited again. "It would actually be in their best interest to have a place like that. Somewhere for the rabble to go, to stay away from tourists, and stop us from being so contrary in front of them. The existence of Vineland benefits everyone."

Her enthusiasm was infectious, but Dana couldn't stop worrying.

"Still..." Dana said. "It's illegal to move without alerting Populace Control. What if they find out what we're doing and have us arrested or put in some dark hole for the rest of our lives?" There were more than enough stories about locals who didn't obey the Tourism Laws and had to be rehabilitated, or sent to detention centres, or forced to work in mines, never seeing the sunlight ever again. Did she really want to risk her comfortable life for something that didn't exist?

"And what if we're very, very careful and we don't get caught?" Jocelyn's eyes pleaded with her. "Haven't you ever wanted more than this? Haven't you ever wanted to live on your own terms?"

Dana frowned. Honestly, she'd never thought of a life other than this one. Sometimes she'd dream about what it would be like to live somewhere not ruled by Govern-Corp, but it was a pipe dream – something that would never happen. She didn't have rich relatives who could sponsor a move off the island, and she'd never be able to save up enough, so why bother dreaming about it?

Although she still had her doubts, Dana had a feeling that Jocelyn would try to find Vineland no matter what. If she agreed to this crazy plan, then at least she could try to keep Jocelyn safe.

Maybe they'd discover that Vineland actually did exist. And if it didn't, at least they'd still be together.

Dana sighed. "You have to promise me that you'll be careful? That we'll be careful?"

Jocelyn's eyes lit up. "I promise."

©

It was all going according to plan, until Jocelyn fell ill. One day she was fine, and the next she was in the hospital with Viral Strain 14. Dana had no idea how it happened or how she'd avoided getting the virus as well, but even though the doctors explained that VS-14 only affected a small percentage of the population, Dana was too paranoid to be comforted.

Had Govern-Corp somehow realized what they were planning? Had Jocelyn said something to the wrong person? Asked the wrong question? Drawn attention to herself?

They'd spent the past five months slowly gathering supplies and information, even going on camping trips in Gros Morne to account for the purchase of certain items, like lamps and bedrolls and backpacks. Dana didn't think that they'd done anything out of the ordinary, but how could she really know?

It was possible that she was overthinking this. Jocelyn's illness could very well have been natural. It might have happened no matter what.

Then again, it wasn't unusual for Govern-Corp's enemies to come down with life-threatening illnesses. There were twenty-three Viral Strains on record, and almost every person who'd passed away from them had been known trouble-makers. Had Jocelyn's name found her way on one of Govern-Corp lists? Was Dana's name also on a list?

Jocelyn had tried to calm Dana's fears, but both of them knew that Jocelyn would never leave the hospital. As the hours passed, she grew sicker and sicker, and nothing the doctors did seemed to make any difference.

Throughout Jocelyn's quick and deadly illness, Dana had to pretend to be a friend and was only allowed to visit during general visiting hours. Whenever she complained about how unfair it was, which was a lot, Jocelyn would smile and tell her to "play the game." More than ever

Dana wished that there wasn't a game to play.

She hadn't been there at the end, which was one of her biggest regrets. She should have tried harder or made up some kind of lie. Even though she knew that Jocelyn wouldn't want her to take unnecessary risks, Dana wished that she'd been there.

She could still hear Jocelyn's last words to her, echoing inside her head. "Be happy," Jocelyn had said, but that seemed impossible now. Dana had no idea what she was going to do without her. All she could manage was to sit in the apartment they'd once shared and cry.

Her gaze fell on the two backpacks in the corner of the room. If things had gone as planned, Jocelyn and she would leave for Vineland next week, but now that would never happen.

It would make sense for Dana to stay here and continue her life, but in the moment that Jocelyn took her last breath, everything had changed. Dana didn't want this. She didn't want to live in a world where she couldn't hold her partner's hand in public, where she had to hide her feelings and pretend to be 'normal', all because some corporation was afraid that her actions might cause controversy. She wanted to live somewhere where she could stay by her partner's hospital bed day and night, where she didn't have to be so afraid.

Wiping the tears from her eyes, she stood up and walked over to the backpacks.

©

This was the part Dana was most afraid of. This was where everything could go terribly wrong.

There weren't many other cars on the highway this late at night. With the high cost of gas, vehicle registration, and licence fees, most people couldn't afford to drive. The only reason Dana had a car was because her parents had gifted it to her before retiring in Twillingate. She'd never bothered to drive it before meeting Jocelyn, but it had become integral to their plan.

Outside Corner Brook, she stopped at a gas station along the highway to purchase a snack and fill up the tank before continuing on. She felt strangely calm, but as she took the turn towards the Port au Port Peninsula, her stomach filled with a horde of nervous butterflies.

Twenty minutes after the turn off, she reached the spot. Taking in a deep breath, Dana pressed down on the gas pedal. She turned the wheel sharply to her right before slamming on the brakes and swinging the wheel to the left. The car sped across the highway and drove off the road, heading for the trees. As the car bounced and jumped over the uneven terrain, Dana was glad she'd tightened her seatbelt, although that didn't stop her head from taking a nasty bump against the door. Luckily the airbags deployed as soon as the front of the car crashed into a tree.

When it was all over, Dana sat in the car for a few minutes, trying to pull herself together. Her body felt sore and shaken, but she could still wiggle her fingers and toes, and her arms and legs worked. Her head hurt, but at least it was still on her neck.

Unbuckling her seatbelt, she opened the door and spilled out on to the ground. There were so many aches and pains that she was afraid to stop and list them, lest she be here for days. Pulling herself up onto her feet, she leaned against the car for a few seconds before moving on with the plan.

Opening the back door, she pulled off the blanket cov-

ering the two backpacks and removed everything from
the car. If the information Jocelyn had gathered was correct, then she should have more than enough provisions
to make the journey. She rolled up the blanket, shoved it
into one of the backpacks, and shut the door.

When someone inevitably found her car, hopefully
they'd assume that she'd gone off the road accidentally,
wandered into the woods while disoriented, and died of
exposure. It was common for people to crash while trying to avoid hitting moose or other animals. Besides, who
would fill up a gas tank before purposefully crashing their
car – especially at these prices?

After checking that there was nobody else on the highway, she turned on her flashlight and looked towards the
woods. Vineland was supposed to be hidden in there,
somewhere. Hopefully it was. Hopefully she wouldn't die
out here alone.

There was still time for her to give up, to stop this crazy plan, ditch the backpacks, and stay with the car. Someone would find her and bring her back to Corner Brook.
She could go back to the life she knew and learn to cope,
learn to adjust. Learn to settle for less.

But Dana didn't want that. She didn't want to bow
down to a corporation that cared more about lining its
pockets than the people who worked for it. She wanted
revenge, she wanted happiness, she wanted freedom...

She wanted more.

Shouldering the backpacks, she walked towards the
woods.

Shannon K Green

A gifted author with a talent for the strange, Shannon Green has been recognized in both the genre community and the contemporary literary community for his pursuits. He was shortlisted for the 1996 Arts and Letters Award, and later won the 2015 Audience Choice Steampunk Newfoundland Showcase.

Green's short fiction has appeared in *Fantasy from the Rock, The Hamthology, Jibbernocky,* and the bestselling collections *Chillers from the Rock, Dystopia from the Rock, Flights from the Rock* and *Pulp Science-Fiction from the Rock.*

He brings with him two new fantasy short stories, 'Pussiedon's Wisdom' and 'Mimir.'

Pussiedon's Wisdom

Tail swishing angrily, Captain Fluffybottom strode across the deck of Pussiedon's Wisdom stroking her whiskers and shouting instructions to her crew. "Get that cargo lashed down! Loose those cables! Hoist the anchor! If you lubbers don't work any faster we'll lose the tide!" She paused as a tom on the wharf caught her attention. "What the devil are you doing holding my gangplank you hangashore?"

The tom removed his hat, scratching one ear as he did so before saying "Captain Fluffybottom, I'm Rutherford Peony. I've been told you might be sailing towards Whisker Bay and I was hoping you'd grant me passage."

"Aye, we sail for Whisker Bay as soon as these layabouts get the lines off!" The last part she shouted to the crew which was busily doing just that. "And that plank is about to be taken in so you've no time to come aboard and discuss passage. Now step away."

"I'll pay whatever you wish," Rutherford said grabbing the rope rails of the gang. "And I'm all ready to sail, everything I need is in my bag." He gestured with a small duffle in his paw. "There is some urgency for my journey."

"Fleeing the port? Best not be running from the

Queen's men if you're looking for passage with meself," the captain replied, as she began untying the ropes on the gangplank. "I'll harbour no such gadabouts aboard me ship."

Rutherford looked back over his shoulder "Not the Queen's men, or the Queen herself. Just an angry husband, and I've litter mates in Whisker Bay."

A growling in the distance began to increase in volume.

Fluffybottom studied the fear on Rutherford's face and scented that it was genuine a heartbeat before she caught sight of the largest feline she could remember seeing prowling up the warf, mouth open and scenting the air. "I didn't know she'd mated to a lynx, for Bast's sake just let me aboard. I'll pay twenty caplin and mop the decks, just don't let that half civilized tom get hold of me."

Fluffybottom nodded, "Aye, grab the end o' the gang and haul." Turning her head to the ship's deck she shouted "Alright b'ys, shove off and hoist the jib soon's as we clears this dock! Our sole passenger has some urgent need of the sea beneath his paws!"

As the vessel swung free on the ebbing tide, the scarred, tawny cat with black tufted ears stopped in the space which had so recently been occupied by the gangplank and Rutherford Peony. Making the connection between the departing ship and the rapid ending of the scent he yowled his frustration to the waves and sky.

Captain Fluffybottom stood at the bow watching large, black thunderheads roll towards the Wisdom and debated how best to tell her passenger that they may need to make port in an unscheduled manner along the way. Given how he'd come aboard, and given the fact that Rutherford had spent the bulk of the last three days either below decks or with his head hanging over the aft rail she didn't think he'd mind. Some of the crew might hiss about the delay but she knew they'd prefer that to being awash in a storm.

That'll be a problem for when he comes out of his bunk, she thought, as she made her way back to the helm and told her second mate "Three points to starboard, there's a harbour where we should be able to ride out the weather if I'm remembering it rightly."

"Aye, captain. Storm really look that bad?" the calico tom asked shifting his weight against his peg as he changed course.

Fluffybottom tugged the gold hoop in what remained of her right ear, she'd lost the top of the ear to a party of boarders years before. "Might be nothing, but it looks like a good deal more than that. Last time I saw clouds like that The Calisto and all hands were lost. Tell the crew we're taking a rest day for the passenger and to splice any port lines t'were damaged with our abrupt departure from Cod Harbour. Give 'em all a tot o' rum once we're at anchor too."

"Aye, Captain. Should I wake the mate and cook as well?" he replied smoothly.

She paused a moment and considered, "Nay, stay the course. I'll send the cabin boy to tell Friendly and tell Cook to make extra scran meself, was headed to me breakfast anyways."

Minutes later, with the first mate roused and the crew preparing for inclement weather, Rutherford emerged from below decks eating a ship's biscuit. "What news Captain?" he asked in much steadier tones than he'd been able to muster in previous days.

"There's a storm blowing our way, we're going to harbour nearby until she passes. Found your sea legs then, have you?" she replied.

"Yes, I always need a day or two. Normally I travel with some cannabis or ginger to ease the symptoms but given the," he paused awkwardly "Let's say, hasty manner in which I left port I didn't have time to replenish my supplies." He examined the approaching clouds. "I say, those clouds do seem to be coming up rather quickly, will we find a harbour before it hits us?"

"It'll be a might close thing, but once we're full head about we'll be running ahead o' it. It'll push to safe anchorage but a few days sail once we try to resume the course," scanning the deck she continued "The wife of a lynx? How'd ye manage that then?"

Rutherford rubbed his ear in a smug manner before answering "A gentleman doesn't kiss and tell. I will say that when not adjusting to the heaving of a ship this cat's tongue is often considered to be silver. Besides, I've never met a feline that didn't appreciate the finer things in life: a compliment on a lovely coat, such as the beautiful garment you wear or that eye catching chapeau; or simple honest gratitude for a job well done, as when I thank the serving wench in a tavern. There are more ways to turn a lady's nose than a dog has fle…"

Fluffybottom cut him off "So you just talk her out of her dress, an' her wit' a big strapper like that at home?"

"Well, he was supposed to be out fishing. At least she said he was," he looked at the clouds, now behind them but coming ever closer. "I say, is that another vessel coming ahead of those storm clouds?"

As the captain turned the sailor in the crow's nest called "Sails to aft, and land 'ho."

"Blast and bother it," Fluffybottom shouted. "Drop

anchors! First watch, prepare boarding parties! Second watch make ready for the storm!" She glared about the deck. "Rutherford, rouse the third mate and tell 'em to get ready for all o' it."

The passenger snapped a salute that Fluffybottom thought was standard amongst cavalry soldiers and hurried off below decks.

Pulling an eyeglass from a sheath at her belt, she surveyed the approaching ship. Seeing the deck littered with poorly shipped nets and crewed by fishercats in fine keep she assumed the approaching vessel to be a trawler crew seeking shelter from the oncoming storm.She wouldn't let her crew know that until she was sure but it allowed her to relax knowing it wasn't corsairs or privateers. While she had no reason to fear the Queen's crews, she didn't like having them aboard, and open pirates were just plain trouble. The name "Bast's Bounty" was painted in a ribbony script on the bow of the approaching ship, furthering her opinion of it being simply a fisher crew seeking shelter from the storm. All about her she could hear the sounds of her crew going about their work: lashing down deck loads; furling sails; battening hatches; and the rattle of sabres and cutlasses as the boarding and repelling crew took position on the starboard rail facing the oncoming vessel.

"Captain," the first mate said in efficient tones at her ear. "The harbour's well sheltered and has a sandy beach. Should we tie up to the shore or drop all anchors?"

"Drop all anchors, Friendly" the captain replied. "Time permitting we'll take short walks ashore when the storm passes. I'll not risk the Wisdom's decks to such clouds as those, nor her hull to an unknown shore. Ye've decided these're harmless fishercats on approach too then?"

He nodded, "Aye, they're flying Queen's colours, but no real flag. Just poor fisherfolks running from the wind. They've not signalled, but alls I've seen is them preparing for the storm."

"Same as meself. If'n we're set to face the gale? Shuffle crew as ye see fit. Clouds such as that at this time o' year we could be here for a few days."

Rutherford cleared his throat at her other side, "Ah, as for me Captain?"

"Ye're cargo for now," she responded as the Bounty dropped anchor on the other side of the harbour and ran up a green flag, the accepted signal of peace on the Catnip Coast.

The storm howled like a she-cat in heat for three days and blew over like a tom scattered by a well aimed boot in the early hours of the fourth. No crew were lost, but the water supplies had begun to taste distinctly salty to the captain and some of her more fastidious crew. Fluffy-bottom set Friendly to work getting the Wisdom ready to sail again and prepared to make land in search of fresher water. From the crow's nest she heard the not unexpected call of "Ahoy Bounty's boat!"

From off to starboard came the return "Ahoy Wisdom, we've fish to trade for tar. The Bounty has taken a slight spring, if ye follow."

Friendly looked to his Captain, she simply nodded. "Aye, we've tar and able hands to apply it should ye need that too. And while we wouldn't say no to some vittles we'd no demand 'em neither. We'll behave civil so long as we've the extra cargo aboard."

Confident that the first mate had matters well in hand Fluffybottom made her way to the Wisdom's boat where she was unsurprised to see Rutherford waiting by the ladder. "Permission to join the shore party, Captain?" he asked. "I might be of no use beyond assistance in the conveyance of…"

She lashed her tail, frustrated with the flowery long-winded speeches her passenger was prone to, "Only if you promise to limit yerself to the minimum number of words needed to cuss at a heavy water cask. I swear I've not met a tom so enamoured with his own yowl since I served under Admiral Trafalger."

Rutherford's only response was "Thank you, Captain," as he shimmied down the ladder and took a seat in the small craft they would be taking to the shore. Fluffy-bottom followed him down, took her customary seat in the bow, and nodded for the oarscats to row them ashore.

The island seemed no different than any of the others dotting the shoreline of the Catnip Coast, Sandy beach, evergreen trees standing alongside palms and birch as they only seemed to in this odd intersection of a northern landmass receiving a tropical current. The captain knew that any crew not actively seeking freshwater would begin ferrying whatever berries and coconuts they found back to the Wisdom as soon as they could. Her crew maximized any opportunity to save money on supplies as it allowed them all a bigger cut of the take on the trade the vessel did.

The party separated by pairs and trudged inland, Rutherford volunteering to walk with Fluffybottom. A situation she found agreeable as she could keep an eye to the scallywag she'd taken aboard, and it would keep him away from some of the younger, more impressionable, lasses in her crew. She was surprised when he said simply, "So all that catnip in the holds, it'd be a shame if somebody told Queen Katmandu about that."

"The what?" Fluffybottom responded with a barely concealed hiss.

"The unstamped 'nip that fills your holds in cleverly boxed bales. The unregulated catnip that has never officially been given leave to depart from Cod Harbour. The catnip which still probably bears the stamp of the excise offices of Her Royal Highness. It would probably not go very well were word that a former Captain of the fleet, Trafalgar's disgraced protégé no less, was in possession of a sizeable quantity of Her Majesty's catnip after a recent theft from the Royal Warehouses," he purred softly.

Fluffybottom turned to give Rutherford a steady glare. "I assure you that everything in my holds has been inspected by the proper tax and excise authorities."

"And some capelin went into their paws so they wouldn't look too closely, didn't it?" Rutherford retorted. "I've been tracking the losses at Her Majesty's personal request for months. You've hidden it well but Whiskers and Mittens rolled over on you after some gentle persuasion. Once we hit Whisker Bay it'll go much easier on you if you come to the Kennel with me without having to be leashed."

Eyes slitted, Fluffybottom bared the claws on her right forepaw as she gripped her cutlass with her left. "And why would ye dream o' making such an offer here, on this forgotten island in the middle o' nowhere? Seems a poor choice for any o' the Queen's Trackers to try and out a smuggler like me."

"So, you don't deny it then?" he purred.

"Nor do I admit to such a ridiculous thing, but bein' accused o' such do make me tail bristle and I'll have satisfaction one way or t'other afore we head back to Pussiedon's Wisdom," she hissed. "Ye says two kittens have named me smuggler and that's enough for a Tracker to lift me, but not in any o' the Queen's ports, so what's yer game tom? Is this how ye talked the lynx's mate inta yer bed?"

Baring his claws Rutherford began to circle slowly, "No, that was all through the power of persuasion. This is a chance to let you play for the freedom of your crew, I know that some of them have to be guilty too, but we just need one cat to blame for the losses Her Majesty has suffered. I understand free enterprise and independence, I'm a modern feline after all, but somebody has to go away to show that Queen Katmandu is still in charge. How else will she hold the army together? How else can we hold the wolves at bay?"

"Ye'll not do it at my expense," she growled drawing her cutlass and lunging towards him. Before she had completed her first step arrows rained down between them.

A small clowder of floppy eared and hairless cats dressed in the uniforms of The Cathgian Empire emerged from the trees. "Hairy ones be silent," the one Fluffybottom assumed to be their leader growled. A gesture at his followers sent them scrambling towards the two would be combatants, lashing the paws of the furry cats behind their backs with a rough rope made of coarsely braided grass.

"I'll settle with ye yet, Rutherford," Fluffybottom hissed.

One of the hairless cats struck her with a bow and shouted "Hairy one, quiet!" The leader of the party turned the group inland, waving anxiously for all to follow.

The group marched through the forest as fast as the restraints on the prisoners allowed. At first Rutherford kept up a string of questions, but was eventually silenced with a quick paw to the snout from one of the hairless cats. Fluffybottom, a little more familiar with the routine of similar groups that inhabited the coast hissed "They won't talk 'til we get ta their leader. Most only got a few words of the Queen's speech." She snapped her jaws shut in a furious snap as a paw was raised towards her.

The rest of the march was conducted in silence until they crested a rise overlooking a small bay on the other side of the island. Rutherford and Fluffybottom gasped in near unison as they took in the three warships at anchor a short distance from the tide line. Neither of them noticing that they had stopped in their tracks until they felt a bow shaft across their shoulders pressing them forward. The leader of the Carthgians spoke a quick command, sending a runner forward as the rest continued their steady pace towards a pavilion on the beach.

Cathgians separated from the group as the proceeded through the camp until there were only two marching the pair of Piscean felines towards the pavilion. Towards whoever commanded this small fleet resting in the harbour.

"Oh, dear sweet mother Bastet," Rutherford spit drawing up short of the pavilion. "That can't be your commander?"

The leader cat shoved Rutherford forward, "Admiral waits. She commands Cathgian fleet here."

"Another lady-cat ye've talked away from her mate?" Fluffybottom snorted in amusement.

"Worse," he responded with a deep sigh. "Far worse."

"Rutherford! You mate stealing son of a dog!" the officer in the pavilion growled as she rose to her feet. "I told you before that if I ever saw your mate stealing, furry tailed waste of rotten food face again you'd be fed my cutlass. Give me one good reason not to bob your tail and clip your ears."

"You stole her mate too?" Fluffybottom asked in a shocked voice.

Head lowered, trying to hide from the full view of the admiral Rutherford whispered "Yes, though the ease with which he came to me makes me think it would have been a short time before he left her anyway. It was part of a mission for Katmandu but one I'll not deny enjoying. Just protect me from her and I'll forget the Queen's 'nip in your hold."

"Very well," Fluffybottom said quietly before straightening and raising her voice. "Admiral of The Cathgian Fleet, I am Captain Fluffybottom of the merchant ship Pusseidon's Wisdom. We sail from the Kingdom of Piscea and are loyal subjects of Queen Katmandu. Whom do I address?"

"I am Admiral Carey of the Cathgian Empire. Commander of the Fleet assigned jurisdiction of the this stretch of the Catnip Coast under the royal imperative of his highness Emperor Napolion, first of his name, long may he rule," the cat responded in more civil tones. "You're far from normal ports for a Piscean captain. What brings you so far from your agreed routes Fluffybottom? Or does Katmandu allow her seafarers such leeway in their navigations as to allow them to stray into waters belonging to others?"

"Admiral, we sought a port to ride out the storm, naught more," Fluffybottom replied her normal accent creeping back into her voice. "Then we thought to take on water before settin' back ta sea. We be simple citizens and traders, not enlisted crew."

"And yet you sail with a known agent of the Queen?" the Admiral asked swishing her tail behind her.

"Well, when I took 'un in I thought he was a rich gadabout in desperate need of passage away from a lynx who was willing to pay triple the normal fare. Now that I knows he's a Queen's man his fare may well go up," Fluffybottom replied. "Or he might spend the last o' his nine 'tween here and Whisker Bay. But he's my cargo, aye."

Carey's tail began to swish more angrily, "And if I tell you I have a score to settle with him?"

"He still be me cargo, Admiral. Yerself knows the rules o' the sea so well as I: a captain's cargo be theirs, short o' an act o' piracy or war ye can't take him without a bargain, and I'll not sell a cat for any reason. Slavery is a crime in both our nations last I checked."

"Do you really think anybody would investigate a lost merchant's ship, Captain? Simply release the miscreant to me and you can go your way."

"Oh, aye, an' I s'pose ye'd have let us be were he no wi' me," Fluffybottom spat. "Nay Admiral, I'll not take such fishguts from the likes o' ye. Ye've seized a free merchant not a fightin' crew, an' if word o' such treachery from the empire reaches the Queen 'twill mean open war."

The Admiral stroked her whiskers and ears slowly, "You speak truth, you cur. We'll…" Her final words were cut off by the thundering of cannon from the harbour mouth.

Rutherford let out a small cheer once he spotted the green and gold of Sennian banners. No doubt a patrol that thought to take the fleet by surprise.While the Cathgians and Sennians were not at war, they were not entirely at peace either. Fluffybottom, seeing her chance for escape, pounced.

Off balance though she was, she bore Carey to the ground through sheer momentum, getting her teeth around the Cathgians neck as she began to rake the hairless cat with one of her free hind paws.

Rutherford, shocked at the ferocity displayed by the smuggler-captain, sprang to life an instant later. A small hop backwards allowed him to bring his forepaws forward, using the tied pair more like a short club than the limbs he had been born with, he lay about him bringing the two guards low.

The Admiral attempted to hiss something to Fluffybottom, but the captain held too tightly to let the words escape. Fluffybottom loosened her grip as she felt the admiral force herself to go limp. "If you let me live I will see to it that you can leave this camp unhindered," the Admiral said hoarsely. When Fluffybottom only replied with an inquiring chirp the Admiral continued. "Given how you responded to the reservation of Rutherford as an agent of the queen I feel certain that you've no wish to face her patrols. Let me live long enough to defend my fleet and spend my remaining lives with honour and I'll see to it you get the chance to face them wherever you choose."

At this Fluffybottom released her grip entirely and straightened. "And Rutherford wit' me, 'less he wants ta seek passage elsewhere."

"Of course," the Admiral purred as she sliced the bonds which bound Fluffybottom's paws. "Will you want his bonds kept on?"

"I'll take care o' this one, you mind yer crew," Fluffybottom said simply. Admiral and Captain bowed formally before Fluffybottom turned to Rutherford. She had just time to slice the rough rope from his paws before he shouted "Look out!"

Dropping to all fours, Fluffybottom rolled immediately to her back. Just in time to see the Admiral leaping through the space recently occupied by the captain. Her momentum carried her into the paws of Rutherford, who merciless extended his claws, raking the Admirals eyes as he shook free the last of his bonds.

While the Cathgian Admiral writhed in pain, the queen's agent extended a bloody paw to Fluffybottom. "Well captain, do we make for your vessel or stay and help the Sennians? They are considered friends and allies by Queen Katmandu and would probably take it as a favour."

"We make fer ship, I'm no' one fer stabbing sailors in their backs when they're facin' enou' from the front," she said as she started sprinting away from the battle. "Enemy or no' a sailor should get the chance to die aboard and I'll no' hinder that."

The pair crossed the island in short time, with occasional calls for the Wisdom's crew to return to the ship. When they reached the beach, they found the crew waiting by the small launch craft.

"Up oars, back to ship," the Captain shouted as every cat present poured of the gunwales. "To ship, we need ta make sea." She continued as the sound of cannon fire rumbled behind them.

As they grew close enough to make out the decks of Pusseidon's Wisdom the captain could see the crew making read to hoist anchor. "What news captain?" Friendly shouted once they were within hailing distance.

"Cathgians and Sennians on the tail side o' the island," Fluffybottom shouted. "Signal the Bounty, they'll no' want part o' that battle anymore 'n we."

As the crew hoisted the landing craft aboard Friendly

told the captain "Our own crew has just returned from the Bounty and say she's ready to sail."

"Then hoist anchors and make for the open seas," Fluffybottom said.

Friendly stroked his ear "Captain, they've no canon aboard, and there's not a draught o' wind."

"Blast the bothering wind! There's a small fleet o' Cathgians battlin' a larger fleet o' Sennians on t'other side o' this island. I'll no take the chance of one o' 'em deciding ta poke their noses 'round the headland and spot us," the Captain spat.

"Make ready to sail!" Friendly shouted. "Captain, we'll ready for the first breath o' wind, but you know yerself we can't sail without wind. Besides, we fly a merchant flag they'll not attack us. We might need to generate some jetsam if you think they'd board and inspect."

The crew wrestled the anchor aboard with a clang that echoed across the deck. The sails were hoisted to hang limp and unmoving in the still air. Shouts could be heard coming across the water from the Bounty as their crew made similar preparations. Smoke drifted over the island and cannonade thundered a steady rhythm, making the ears of half the cats onboard twitch as they completed their preparations. "Have the watch teams stand ready for possible boarders and the flagman signal the Bounty to see if they'll need assistance. Belay that, send a boat ta the Bounty with crew ta help 'em defend if need be," Fluffybottom commanded.

"And me Captain?" Rutherford, asked from where he stood nearby.

"I'll no' give ye ta the Sennians anymore'n I'd given ye to the Cathgians, Queen's man or no," Fluffybottom said curtly. "I mightn't be in the navy no more but I'll not see the Queen's subjects given ta foreign sailors. As fer after that… We'll have ta wait 'n see."

The boarding party had assembled and begun lowering the boat when the wind rose, filling the sails. "Cancel ship's boats!" Friendly shouted as both the Bounty and the Wisdom began to move slowly out of their harbourage.

"Signal them an offer of escort to Whisker Bay," Fluffybottom said. "And confine Rutherford ta his berth once we're well clear o' the tangle o' this island." She strode to the bow and watched the sea race toward them.

Three uneventful days later the two vessels were tying up in Whisker Bay. In the midst of the hustle and bustle that always accompanies such tasks Captain Fluffybottom took Friendly aside "Yer ta keep Rutherford in his berth 'til the cargos offloaded. After that the Queen's agent may go wherever he likes and the devil take the lying pouncer," she instructed her first mate.

"And if the excise officers come aboard?" Friendly asked.

"Not but two lazy cats in their bunks, or mayhap I'll invent a small infraction yer being punished fer. They'll no wanna talk ta ye any road."

Before the captain had finished her words two very officious looking cats, the larger a ginger and the smaller a calico, hailed the ship from the pier, "Ahoy, Wisdom! We received word the new head of excise and custom for Whisker Bay was aboard. May we speak with him?"

"An' who might he be, then?" Fluffybottom returned.

"One Rutherford Equinox," the smaller of the official cats shouted.

"Tie my whiskers and bob my tail," Friendly cursed.

"Captain?"

"Fetch 'im," Fluffybottom told her tabby first mate. "Come aboard while I have the sluggard fetched, no sea legs ta that one a'tall."

In short order the excise cats were aboard, with a copy of the ship's manifest in paws, and Rutherford was on deck performing introductions between the officials and the ranking members of the crew. "There will be no need to inspect the hold," he told the port agents. "I took the liberty while we sailed. Though I expect you all to dine at my table tonight."

"With pleasure, Rutherford," she said with mild surprise in her voice. "I'll send a few of the lads along with your luggage in short order."

Rutherford stroked his ears as he responded "Given what I came aboard with I doubt that necessary, consider it payment in full for the passage and the shelter from inclement weather. I'll send a messenger to tell you the time and place of the meal.

With that said, he strode down the gangplank with his new underlings in tow. When Captain Fluffybottom inspected the sole piece of luggage her only passenger had brought she found it contained a full change of clothes and a letter stating that the holder was in service to Queen Katmandu and not to be questioned by any in her service.

Mimir

She looked through the narrow gap between the boards on the window. Dust swirled across the landscape obscuring her view of what she knew was a barren wasteland. She felt a small figure rubbing against her leg, the fur soft against the skin bared by the hole in her jeans. "We'll give it a few more minutes then we'll hit the road okay Mister Whiskers," she said quietly. Receiving a quiet purr in answer, the only answer she expected, she turned away from the window to check that she had collected all of her belongings and ready herself for what she knew would be a long, cold march.

She couldn't remember how long it had been since she'd left the community shelter, a week, two maybe? Less than three weeks, certainly. She knew that she had had enough of the backbiting and arguing and general lack of action. They were all content to cower in the old school as the food ran out and no news came in. The radios had stopped working, or the radio stations had stopped broadcasting, which amounted to the same thing. The snow had stopped its constant falling, though it still fell occasionally, and all the sensors they had said the outside world was free of everything they could scan for that was dangerous to human life. The small council which the refugees had elected to govern their affairs had denied any and all possibility of exploration trips, had initially been against even allowing the residents access to areas outside the gymnasium and attached locker rooms in fact. As if anybody among the fifty or so huddled in that gymnasium couldn't manage a stroll to the shopping centre across the road to see if there was any toilet paper or bottled water left. So Mimir had decided it was time to leave the disaster shelter.

She had been on the road for less than a day, enjoying the gentle breeze and unfiltered sunlight, when she heard the distressed cries coming from a group of garbage cans. She had opened a few of the bins before she found it. A small black and grey ball of fluff had leapt from the confines of the trash can as she removed the lid. Content that she had found and freed the distressed animal, Mimir went on her way. She awoke the next morning to the sensation of something tickling her face; the cat curled into the top of her bedroll and brushing her with his whiskers.

The two had continued on their way west together. Sometimes Mister Whiskers would vanish for the majority of the day only to return by the following morning, sometimes with an offering of a dead mouse or bird. Mimir often turned these aside, sometimes she would prepare the offerings to eat; it depended on the state of her supplies and how hungry she was.

There had been little shortage of supplies in the empty houses she found, often more food for her and her rapidly growing companion than she could carry. Sometimes the pair would stop in an abandoned house for a few days to rest. Usually when it looked as if a new storm was blowing through. Mister Whiskers often took the lead when it came to seeking these temporary shelters.

The first time it had happened, he had led her to a largely intact cabin somewhere between the last community they'd been in and the one the kilometer count on road signs kept telling them was getting closer. She had entered mainly to see if there was anything with which she could resupply and discovered a library of fiction and nature handbooks such as one might expect at vacation resort. That night she'd fallen asleep with a guide to wild plants in her hand and on waking the next day had found a raging blizzard outside. After that she paid more attention when the no-longer-a-kitten left for his little jaunts.

After a few more brief stops Mimir noticed that they had acquired another shadow. At first Mister Whiskers would growl at the stranger's approach, but it remained, hovering at the edge of the firelight at night. Sometimes, if they slept inside, the new member of the band could be seen peering through the windows or be heard just outside the door. Nothing more than a pair of glowing green eyes in the gloom. Eventually a larger tabby with a notched ear could be seen just inside the firelight. Mimir decided his name was Oscar, after a character she had seen in a book in one of the houses she had weathered a storm in.

The newly formed trio continued on, more westward than any other direction. Making their way as far as they felt comfortable during the day. Spending the nights in abandoned cars, or houses, or the small tent Mimir carried on her back. When food was scarce, they went hungry. When they were cold, they huddled together. When snows fell, they sought someplace dry to sleep.

They had been staying in a small cottage near a lake for few days. Mimir and the others merely enjoying the warming weather, when they heard a sound like thunder in the clear skies. The ice on the nearby river was breaking, the waters rising behind and sweeping into the small lake. Mister Whiskers ran back to the cottage they had adopted as their own while Oscar ran towards the torrent flowing towards them. Mimir chased him, intent on saving the cat from his own foolhardiness when she heard what he must have been running towards: the cries of kittens.

She saw them finally, stranded on an upper floor of one of the neighbouring out buildings. Mimir examined the newly expanded banks of both the lake and its tributary river. She saw no clear path to the defenseless babes but could hear the cries of a larger cat with them, possibly the queen. Hoping they would be okay for the short term began to seek a way to the small clowder. Near one of the cabins she found a small canoe, but was unsure how to pilot the unfamiliar conveyance. There was a rope in the canoe however, and she did know many ways in which she could use that.

Tying one end of the rope to the porch rails of the cottage and the other around her waist, she grabbed what she thought was the front of the canoe and began to wade towards the stranded kittens. The flood made the going slow, but fortunately wasn't quite deep enough to totally impede her progress.

When Mimir reached the cottage with the kittens she tied the canoe to the steps and tried the door only to find it locked, but Oscar scrambled from beneath one of the seats and through a window beside the door. Mimir struggled to reach through the window eventually managing to get the door open. Snatching a blanket from the couch in the front room, she climbed the stairs to find Oscar squared off against the largest female she had ever seen. Without thought she threw the blanket over the queen and formed it into a bundle which she flung over her shoulder. Next, she swept the kittens into a drawer from a nearby night stand and rushed back down the stairs.

Outside the water had risen but she carefully placed her cargo into the canoe and began pulling on the rope which she had tied to the nearby cottage. With help from the flood waters the group soon reached their make-shift pier and unloaded from their small vessel. Mimir scrambled the small group toward the cottage she had been using, the cat in the blanket hissing and clawing the whole way. Flood waters nipping at her heels she made it to the cottage her small family had been using, which she'd selected because the rise it was on gave her a better view of the recently frozen lake. She took the drawer and bundled blanket into a back room on the second floor and closed the door.

With the new comers settled Mimir set about preparing the cottage to withstand whatever flood may be coming. She gathered all her belongings, moved them to one of the unused rooms upstairs, and changed out of her wet clothes. Then she gathered everything else she thought she could use; food items, blankets, extra pillows; and moved that into the neighbouring upstairs rooms. Last she carried as many books up the stairs as she could. She lamented the possible loss of the fireplace, but had assembled a number of candles and a pot large enough to hold a small fire if she was careful. When she finally settled down to a small meal of cold canned beans, she saw that Mister Whiskers and Oscar had prepared for the flood in a similar manner. They had carried a small collection of crumpled paper balls they used as toys, blankets, and pillows to the door of the room where Mimir had sealed the queen and her kittens. It seemed the pair were taking turns to sit at the top of the staircase, keeping the water from entering the house. The lapping of the water at the walls of the cottage lulled them all to sleep.

The next day Mimir awoke to scratching at the door of the sealed room. She opened the door and let the mother cat out. Gently it brushed her leg before fleeing down the stairs. Mimir followed her to the lower floor, surprised to see no traces of water having invaded her temporary home. Looking out the window she was more surprised to see that the house was now completely surrounded by water. While waters lapped at the front of the house the back of the house was clear for perhaps a dozen yards before the newly isolated point became an island. Mimir let the new cat out and, leaving the door open, followed her into the cool morning. The queen quickly searched out the limits if their new land and began searching for something at the water's edge.

Mimir gathered some wood from the pile near the back door, went back inside the house, and lit a fire. She put fresh bowls of water and food out for the cats and settled down to absorb some of the warmth of the fire. It was a pleasant morning, despite the heavy mists outside and the coziness of her private island paradise was welcome.

Later in the day Mimir set about making the little cottage secure. She braced the walls as best she could to prevent any ingress of water. Then she transported everything she had left on the lower floor to the upper floor, sorting it between the rooms as she might need it. She made a makeshift litter box for the cats in the washroom. She even found a portable barbecue where she could burn wood or the scanty supply of coal she found in the cabin to cook over should the flood waters rise. She knew she would be here until the waters receded or the kittens had weaned and were old enough to travel.

Mister Whiskers and Oscar kept their split watch over the kittens while their mother came and went at her leisure, only settling with the kittens long enough for them to feed. Mimir had just finished hanging her wet clothing around the fire when she heard loud cries and hisses coming from behind their shelter. She ran to the back door, afraid that the cats were fighting.

When she looked out of the open doorway she saw that they were indeed fighting, but not each other as she had feared. An otter had swum up on their little shoreline and was trapped between Oscar, the new queen, and now, her. The queen darted towards the otter with a speed that rivaled the fastest runner Mimir had ever seen, claws hooking at the otter's eyes. The otter tried to run in Oscar's direction but he simply flicked a paw at the otter turning it back. Again, the queen's claws flashed towards the otter, who turned, this time towards Mimir. She threw a piece of firewood at it, turning it back towards the water.

But the new cat, this nursing queen, was not satisfied to see the otter in full flight towards the open water. She jumped onto its back, sunk her teeth into the otter's neck and began to furiously scratch with her hind legs. She only let go when the otter fully submerged itself in the water. Anger clear on her face the queen swam ashore and began to lick herself clean. "I think you must be called Thresher," Mimir said to her. "Like the machines that gouged the ground in the time when people still farmed."

For the first day after that Mimir made a point of watching whenever the cats went outside, fearful of the damage that might befall them unsupervised, but the next day she realized this was foolishness when Thresher brought in a large trout, followed by a very smug looking Mister Whiskers carrying another. Mimir dutifully cleaned the fish, cooked one for herself and split the other for all the cats. The kittens were now beginning to wander the room which she had set aside for them and were still nursing but sniffed and licked at the pieces they were offered.

The next few days passed peacefully. Mimir read while the cats stalked the edges of their small island. The waters rose and fell without regularity. Occasionally large pieces of wood washed ashore, to be pulled near the little cottage and split for firewood. Another day the mostly de-cayed carcass of some large animal washed ashore. Mimir suspected it might have been one of the feral cows which now roamed the landscape, she pushed it back out into the water as quickly as she could; but not before Thresher and Mister Whiskers had managed to take a taste of the unknown animal. Mimir spent the next day nursing the pair back to health. After that none of the cats would eat anything that they didn't kill on their own or receive from Mimir.

By the time the waters had receded enough that their island seemed part of the coastline again, the troop of kittens were fully weened and eating solid foods. Mimir collected what she could from the neighbouring cottages and headed westward once more. The days blended one into the next. The kittens learned how to hunt from Os-car, how to find shelter from Mister Whiskers, and how to fight from Thresher.

They had been travelling for a week or so, Mimir wasn't sure, when they were awakened by the sound of disturbance in their camp. A large four-legged creature with uneven horns jutting from its head was rummaging through Mimir's pack. Thresher wasted no time in charg-ing the feral bull, howling, and leaping straight for its face. Oscar and Mister Whiskers lead the not quite kittens in a flanking manoeuvre, mercilessly raking the sides of the bull with their claws before further dividing to attack the confused creature's stomach and back while some maintained the harassment from the flanks. Mimir, shocked at their reaction only hesitated a moment before grabbing her spear and adding her own efforts to the attack,

The bull bellowed, roaring its rage and disbelief to the lonely clearing before being borne to the ground by the relentless attacks of Mimir and her clowder. Quietly she slit the throat of the beast and let it bleed out. The cats lapped the blood like it was the freshest cream. The group ate their fill of stringy beef that night and did their best to preserve what they could not immediately use.

After nearly three months of travel, three days after the incident with the bull, Mimir finally found what she sought, another settlement. She knew they existed but had been unsure as to where they might be. They greeted her as a stranger, the first they'd seen since the troubles had caused everybody to seal themselves in the shelters, but were willing to trade for the extra meat she carried and to learn what news she had. The mayor of the town gave her a copy of his map of the known shelters in their state and offered her a position as chief hunter for the small community.

She declined the offer, fearing a repeat of the shelter she had left, and moved to the nearest shelter on the map. It was then she noticed that kilometers had been replaced by miles on all the road signs she passed, she hadn't noticed the change focused as she was on watching the numbers change. It was late afternoon of her second night back on the road when she found the barn.

There was nothing on her map indicating that people lived nearby, neither a refugee camp or a former town but the large red structure loomed above the skeletal trees looking every bit the haunted mansion she had seen in the many story books she had read. The paint, at one-point red, now faded to a dull pink where it hadn't flaked from its walls. The partially snow-covered roof, missing shingles in some places and moss covered in others. Even the pair of high, evenly spaced gable windows peering out over the surrounding wooded area screamed stay out to Mimir. Naturally, Thresher and Oscar darted through the trees and through the partially open door. With a sigh Mimir followed them, Mister Whiskers and the kittens joining her as she crossed the threshold.

The only tracks in the low drift of snow which extended from door into the barn bore only the familiar tracks of her two wayward felines she noted with some relief. The air felt still to her after the long march outside, but the sparkle of hay dust in the odd shafts of weak sunlight told her the lie of that. Lowering the hood of her jacket she inhaled the scent of old, damp hay and moldy wood. Not the best place she had been led by the by the cats, but far from the worst.

Laying her backpack aside she made her way deeper into the building. The dying light revealed the interior of the building to be less than it had appeared from the exterior, nothing more than an empty barn in surprisingly good upkeep. The sound of rats squealing as the clowder went to work in earnest told her all she needed to know about the possibility of spending the evening here, it would do.

After preparing one of the stalls as a sleeping area Mimir went outside seeking firewood. Instead she found a young man holding a rifle. "What you think you're doing here?" he asked in a voice choked with fear.

"Spending the evening in an abandoned barn," Mimir

replied calmly. "I didn't think anybody would mind."

"Well it isn't abandoned, it's mine," he said from behind the shaking rifle. "Who told you that you could sleep here?"

Doing her best to keep her own fear out of her voice Mimir responded "Nobody said I could, like I said I didn't think anybody would mind. I mainly just wanted a night under a roof, the cats and I will be gone in the morning."

"Cats? Honest to goodness cats?" he asked, some excitement creeping into his voice. One of the kittens, all tawny stripes, drawn by the voices poked its head through the doorway.

Laying the gun down the young man crouched and called the it to him. "You are a handsome kitty, yes you are. Why you traveling with this lady, huh? Is she good people little kitty?" he said as he scratched the now loudly purring cat under its chin.

"I think that answers that question about both of us," Mimir said relaxing.

"How'd you find us, we're a ways off the main track?" the young man asked continuing to pet the small cat before him.

"The clowder led me here, I think they were attracted to the easy prey in the barn. Might be they just wanted a night out of the cold," she said. "Can we stay or do I need to get back on the road?"

He eyed her slowly. "You can stay in the barn, nothing else using it besides the rats and maybe some squirrels since the last horse died," he replied. "But you're going to have to pay for it somehow."

Seeing the woman turn pale he quickly added "I mean with a can of food or something, it doesn't have to be much. Just that I got a wife to answer to and other mouths to feed."

"I do have some fairly fresh jerky, maybe some apples," Mimir paused and thought. "Of course, my cats will probably have killed all the rats in the barn by morning. That should be worth at least half a night inside."

He smiled and put out his hand "Deal, it might not feed anybody but at least we'll be clear of the varmints." They shook and he walked away as snow started to fall. "Course, if the weather is bad in the morning you can stay on, but make sure your kitties get all of them rats."

She thanked him, collected enough deadfall for a small fire and returned to the barn. The next morning dawned behind a bluster of snow. Mimir stretched in the chilly air of the barn and wrapped herself in an old horse blanket she found in one of the stalls, trying not to disturb the cats around her. Only dragging herself from her nest when she heard a voice at the door.

"You awake, ma'am?" a woman called. At a grunt from Mimir the voice continued. "One of your cats made its way to our door last night and I wanted to make sure you were all warm enough out here."

Mimir strode to the door, clutching the blanket tightly about herself. "I've been in worse," she answered with a yawn. I made use of the old blankets I found in here and the hay is more comfortable than the cots we had at the shelter where I used to live."

"Well J.C. told me about the deal you two struck last night, and I was fine with it before the weather blew in, but now I'd like to change it," the woman began.

"I've nothing else to offer," Mimir interrupted, an edge of panic plain in her voice as she watched the snow swirl outside.

"I want to invite you into the house," the woman cut right back in with a wave of her hand. "Even if you and yours weren't cleaning out this barn for us I wouldn't want anybody out in this mess. All we'll add to the deal is some conversation, maybe some news if your travels gave you any."

Mimir smiled and thanked the woman as the pair made their slow way to the main house. She found that the house was occupied by J.C., his wife Jane, their son Thommy, and Jane's mother Sarah. All but Thommy were hungry for news. All were also excited by the feline visitors, especially the toddler Thommy.

After a small meal of cheese omelettes, over which J.C. explained that this was still a fairly productive dairy farm which produced more than the small family could use, Mimir shared what news she had of the outside world while playing with young Thommy. She was interrupted by a mewing and scratching at the door.

J.C. went to see what the noise was about and returned with the tawny striped cat. "I don't think this one likes to be outside as much as the others," he said with a chuckle. "What's his name?"

Mimir examined the cat before saying honestly, "I don't know. He's Thresher's son but most of her litter don't have names yet."

"Fluffy!" shouted Thommy, reaching for the cat, who ran to the toddler. As the pair rolled together, in a tangle of toddler laughter and cat fur the rest of the room said in near unison "Fluffy."

The rest of the day passed in companionable peace. Fluffy and Thommy napped while the adults prepared meals, washed dished, and fed the small fireplace which heated the house.

She spent two nights with them, then packed her bags to begin visiting the other shelters. Her family had grown but would never be complete until she found her human daughter.

Jeff Slade

A resident of Salmon Cove, Slade is a prize-winning author and avid reader who enjoys both making and hearing puns, playing the guitar, and cats.

Slade has previously been featured in 2018's *Chillers from the Rock* with his short story 'The Culling,' in 2019's *Dystopia from the Rock* with his story 'Anchored,' in *Flights from the Rock* with his story 'Flight of the Puffin,' and in *Pulp Science-Fiction from the Rock* with his story 'The Daring Mid-flight Heist on the Moonbeam Express.'

His award-winning story, 'Extinguished,' was featured in *Kit Sora: The Artobiography*.

Slade brings with him reprints of his original works, the chilling tale 'The Culling' and the science-fiction 'Anchored.'

The Culling

I remember it like it was yesterday.

The three bodies lay spread out in a line before me, each on a wooden table equidistant from the next. They were covered in white sheets from the waist down, bare feet peeking out.

I stood in a small clearing in an unfamiliar wooded area. The only living things in sight were the snow-topped evergreen trees that hemmed the clearing in.

My guardian, Uncle Lachlan, brought me there with a man I didn't know. I only knew he was an invigilator for my final test in becoming a full-fledged member of the coven: the Culling. Anyone with potential in the Art has to go through it on their thirteenth birthday. Instead of blowing out candles on a cake, I was sorting corpses in the woods.

I'd never seen a dead body before that day. I've seen plenty since.

My uncle handed me three coloured stones before they exited the clearing: red, brown, and black for vampire, werewolf, and wight respectively. I ran my thumb across the coloured side of each one before sliding them into the pocket of my burgundy peacoat. The coat clashed with my red hair, but I didn't care; I was a stubborn child.

My task was to place each fist-sized stone -- fist-sized for a thirteen-year-old girl at any rate -- on the foot of the correct table.

It reminded me of pin the tail on the donkey, only much more morbid.

The snow crunched under my feet as I slowly approached the leftmost table. My eyes were transfixed on the table and its previously living contents as I sidled around to the far side, keeping my back to the woods. I peered over the table and forced myself to take in the deceased's features.

Mercifully, the eyes were closed. The man's skin was pale, but not as ashen or gray as one would expect for a wight. His closely cropped black hair formed a widow's peak, pointing where I needed to look.

I cleared my throat, the sound amplified by the snowy silence around me, and stood on my tiptoes. Thankful to be wearing gloves, I placed my fingers on the man's chin and gently pulled downward. Pulling back his lips allowed me to see inside his mouth.

Fangs.

I let go and moved to the foot of the table, brushing off some snow before placing a red stone there.

Without looking back, I started toward the middle corpse. I didn't need to get close; its skin was far more gray and sallow than the previous one, and a quick glance at the third table confirmed its corpse too was lighter than the middle one.

I was anxious; was I about to finish the Culling? I pulled both remaining stones out of my pocket to pick the correct one, accidentally dropping them in the process. I wasn't quite sure what I expected, but I'd thought it'd be harder than that. I kneeled down and plucked the stones out of the snow, taking the black one in my right hand and dropping it onto the end of the middle table as I got to my feet.

When I turned to the empty last table, I froze.

A glance at the brown stone in my left hand reminded me it was the werewolf that had disappeared. Prior to that, I hadn't heard any noises other than my own and the occasional sliding snow off of boughs and branches; certainly nothing that caused any concern for my safety.

Before I could process anything further, I detected movement in my peripheral vision and whirled around. The first corpse, which I'd designated as the vampire, was sitting up and turning to face me, eyes wide open.

I had no weapons, aside from my wits. Those would have to do. I backed up instinctively until I bumped into the empty table, then felt around it in search of something I could use as a weapon. All I came up with was the stone in my hand, and I hurled it at the vampire's head with as much force as I could muster.

It bounced off its upper left temple where it landed, leaving a slight indentation but accomplishing nothing more than that. The vampire grinned and slid off of the table, calmly making its way toward me. It was in no rush.

All I could do was move behind the empty third table. Running through the woods would only slow me down; my clothing would almost certainly catch on the prickly shrubbery and softwood which surrounded me. An ensnarled target would be easy prey for my foe.

I had to think quickly, as the vampire was now standing on the opposite side of the table. I knew I had to attack before it did, so I struck out with the first thing that came to mind. Closing my eyes, I muttered under my breath, raised my fist high and then slammed it downward.

One of the largest nearby trees came smashing down between us as I manipulated the earth below, uprooting and felling it with swift, strong purpose. I closed my eyes at the sound, and when I opened them, I saw the vampire on the other side of the fallen fir.

"Missed," it growled.

Before it could do or say anything else, I leapt into action. The tree might have missed its mark, but it smashed the table between us into pieces. I picked up one of the shards as I ran over the tree branches. I aimed the jagged edge at the vampire's chest and threw all my weight behind it as I lunged forward.

I got back to my feet following the collision. The vampire didn't, a look of surprise permanently frozen on its twice-dead face.

As I brushed pine needles off my coat, a loud groan caught my attention. The wight was shuffling towards me, arms outstretched as it hobbled forward. It probably didn't want to give me a birthday hug.

Raising my arms, I felt my fingers tingle and buzz as I summoned forth a surge of electricity. Thin, powerful lattices of energy arced forward and found their target, stopping the wight in its tracks as it shimmied and shook, smoking in place.

After a few seconds, however, it started moving again. It turned out electricity was not very effective against the undead, shocking as that might sound.

I decided to try something different. Wiping the fresh sweat off my brow, I took a step backwards from the steaming corpse and concentrated once again. Calling upon my dwindling reserves, I flicked my left hand towards my enemy and a bolt of fire sizzled through the winter air towards it.

This attack proved much more effective. The wight

fell to the snow-covered ground, flailing as the flames consumed its dead flesh. As it thrashed around, the fire spread from its arms to the fallen tree.

Smoke from the burning boughs quickly filled the small area, and my eyes started watering. I began coughing. Instinctively I ran for the opposite corner of the clearing until I remembered: there was still one foe remaining.

As if on cue, a large, dark figure flew through the smog. I was able to partly dodge out of the way, but the creature's claws still rendered three parallel gashes through the chest of my coat. I spun and fell onto my back. I wasn't sure if I was bleeding due to the dark burgundy colour of my clothing. I was sure that I would be bleeding imminently, however, if I didn't act fast.

The great lupine shadow that had sailed through the smoke mere seconds ago had turned and was now rounding on me. Its midnight-black fur and bright, sharp fangs, one in stark contrast against the other, became better illuminated by the fire. It paused long enough to snarl at me before it sprang into action, coming to tear out my throat.

I was nearly tapped out from my previous exertions. My hands reached around me, frantically in search of another piece of wood, something, anything to thrust between the animal and myself, but all I found was snow and ice.

Reaching down deep, I depleted the last of my energy and reshaped the surrounding ice with my remaining willpower. Just as the werewolf went airborne, an icy spear thrust out at the base of my feet. Too late to change its course, the beast impaled itself throat-first on the long, pointed shard of frost.

Its dying howl of anger and frustration slid into a warm gurgle, its breath warm and damp against my cheeks only inches away from my face. The werewolf went limp, and

I pulled myself to my feet with a groan.

Exhausted, I surveyed the scene. The fire had died down on both the fir tree and the wight, though the latter was still faintly gasping and wriggling in place. With a sigh, I snapped off the end of the icicle, walked over, and plunged it down and through the wight's blackened forehead.

It stopped wriggling.

I sank to my knees, finally letting my guard down. I lowered my head and frowned at the drops of blood I saw in the snow. There were three drops, followed by a fourth, then a fifth, before I realized the blood was falling from my nose. I wiped it clean, then held my head as a newly discovered headache intensified.

The sound of boots crunching in the snow caught my attention, but I didn't turn around. All three of my enemies were down. If there were more, it didn't matter. I was spent.

"Less than ten minutes total. Impressive," said a male voice I recognized as my guardian's.

"It's impressive she's still alive," another man chimed in. The invigilator, a dim voice in the back of my head reminded me.

"Yes, yes, of course," replied my uncle. He knelt beside me and took a glove off his hand, feeling my forehead. "She'll be fine, she just needs to rest." Leaning in closer still, he whispered under his breath, "Good job, Ryan."

"It seems we have another elementalist on our hands." The other pair of boots scrunched once again as the invigilator examined the carnage. "My gods, Lachlan, can you imagine how powerful she'll be once she's older?"

"Of course," my uncle replied, squeezing my shoulder before returning to a standing position. "That's the plan."

Anchored

Callie traversed through woods that grew more and more unfamiliar with every step. Each twig and branch clumsily snapped underfoot, and she tried not to think about how the noise betrayed her position.

"How far 'way are we now?" asked a voice behind and to the right of her.

"Dunno," Callie replied. "Two days' walk away, however far that is." She'd left home two days earlier with her younger sister, Bree, after their grandmother had moved from the family tent into the hospice tent on the outskirts of the community. The same tent their mother had moved into four years ago, from which she'd never returned.

They walked in near silence for another few minutes, ducking under and pushing away the thick branches and scratchy brambles they encountered the further they went.

"She could'a woke up, y'know," Bree added.

Their grandmother had been sick for some time; while she'd had her good days, they got farther and fewer in between the bad ones, and the bad kept getting badder. One morning she wouldn't wake up; that same morning they brought her to hospice, and they packed up and left camp.

"She's not coming back, Bree." Callie abruptly stopped and turned. Bree bumped into her, then looked up at her, a startled expression swimming to the surface of her face.

"Not like that," Callie snapped. "You know I don't mean like that." Her own face softened, and she stooped down, placing a hand on Bree's shoulder. She smoothed out the thin, well-worn jacket before reaching up and stroking long brown hair that matched her own.

"D'you think she's been anchored yet?"

"I don't know, sweetie." There was no use in lying to her, Callie thought. They only had each other now, after all; they'd never known their father, and neither had their mother, not really. "Probably. But that's for the best, right?"

"Right. So, she can't come back." Bree finally looked up and met her gaze. "I just miss her. And Mom."

"Me too, kiddo." She pulled her sister in for a hug, then kissed the top of her head. "But we've gotta keep moving, okay?"

The smaller girl just nodded and pulled away, wiping her face with the back of her hand. "Where are we goin' again?"

"You remember the story Grandma used to tell us, 'bout the island?" They resumed walking, and Callie resisted the urge to take her sister's hand, not wanting to treat her a child. She knew that she hated that.

"Yeah, where she met Granddad," Bree chimed in, kicking a rock out ahead of them through the brush.

"'Zactly. She used to tell us all the time, when we'd gather 'round the campfire, tryin' to keep warm." Callie's own mind retreated back to the days when she was Bree's age, trying to ignore the never-ending snowfall and the dampness you felt down to the bone. "An' how she took

Ma there when she was small, smaller than us."

"The lights were like fire," said Bree. "And the cotton candy."

"Yeah, movin' so fast, blurrin' together. Red and yellow and orange." Callie had dreamed about the lights countless times. She chuckled as her little sister's mind went to food. "And the cotton candy, yeah. Pink an' fluffy, all you could eat. 'Fore the Awakening," she added.

They walked in silence for another while, letting that hang out in the open without any further comment. Neither of them wanted to linger on that topic for long, not when they both knew where they were headed.

They searched for food along the way, a search that even before leaving home regularly took them deeper and deeper into the forest. Winter was coming, and the overplucked trees and bushes nearest to home - which provided minimal sustenance due to overuse at the best of times - were bare.

Some time later, Bree pointed quietly to a black strip of ribbon that hung from a nearby tree. A warning marker.

"We're almost out of bounds," said Bree. They'd never been out this far before, but they had no choice. There was nothing for them back at the camp now, and besides, the lack of food at home also meant a lack of prey to hunt; a dangerous chain reaction in lack of resources.

Callie stared up at the ribbon as it fluttered in the slight, chilly breeze. The atmosphere was eerily quiet the closer they got to the coastline as what little life that was left steered far clear of the water. The markers were placed to warn you how far from home you were; a green one came first, followed by a yellow, then a red. They'd passed the first two yesterday, and the latter earlier in the morning.

No one was supposed to go past the red marker, and, until today, Callie never had. It was meant to be the absolute limit, the threshold which they should not cross, and it allowed for a safe amount of buffer space between that point in the woods and the shore. She'd heard tell of other markers, but no one could say what colours they were; now she knew.

"We keep going," pronounced Callie, before starting to march forward once more. Bree hesitated but followed, just behind and to one side of her.

Callie winced as her stomach pained, harder than normal. Hunger was the default state for her and her generation, though she'd heard stories of a time when it wasn't. When it was a reminder that you needed to eat, not something you temporarily sated when you were lucky enough to find food.

She didn't believe those stories. They had to be lies.

Pulling her cloak tighter around her, Callie wondered if they'd have to stop and set up camp soon. She had no idea how much further they had to go, but it was getting close to dusk. Soon enough it'd be difficult to build a decent shelter and fire.

Before she could think upon that any further, Bree tapped her on the shoulder and pointed ahead.

"Look," was all her sister managed.

One more marker stood between them and an apparent exit to a clearing ahead. It rose out of the ground, white and bleached, and leaned at a slightly crooked angle, to the left. Callie had no medical training, but it appeared to be a femur.

Beyond the bone marker, the woods gave way and parted open, revealing a sharp drop-off and a view of the horizon, where the ocean met the sky, the sun nearly completely set.

"What's that sound?" asked Bree.

"I don't know," Callie admitted. She looked at her sister, then crept forward, giving the bone marker a wide berth.

The sound grew louder with each step, until she emerged from the woods and stood at the edge of the cliff. Down below, the ocean crashed and pounded into the rocky shoreline, each wet smack ringing in their ears.

Callie looked from one side to the next. They couldn't go down over the cliff, not without hurting themselves, and the left was blocked off by a thick copse of trees. The only way left to go was to the right, so that's where she headed, Bree in tow.

"I don't like this," Bree muttered from her orbit behind Callie.

"Neither do I, but let's stay quiet and see what we can find." They wouldn't get back home now, as they couldn't risk traveling in the dark. Not that there was anything - or anyone - waiting for them back there anyway.

The path stuck close to the shoreline, with a thin strip of beach between them and the water, and a thick wall of trees on their other side. They stayed closer to the woods, careful to avoid the water at all costs, until buildings came into view. Callie stopped, holding a hand out to halt Bree.

"Looks like potential shelter," she said, biting her lip. The sun had fully gone down now, and the blood orange hue in the sky was fading fast. A lone building stood just ahead of them, and what looked like many other similar structures further down the beach.

"Maybe we can camp out there, just for the evening?" Bree asked. "Come, let's check it out."

Something deep inside Callie warned her not to go, to turn around and run, but she chalked it up to the ravenous hunger that was devouring her from the inside out. Besides, there was danger in either option, as the woods were no safe place either, especially at night. At least with the building they'd have walls to surround and hide them, even if they appeared ancient and decrepit.

"Alright, but let me lead." She cautiously approached the building, the only noise the ebb and flow of the tide.

As they drew near, they saw the wooden door to the structure was slightly ajar, creaking back and forth with the breeze. No light emanated from inside, and there were no signs of life. Callie examined the sand all around the building, but there were no footprints nor animal tracks visible either.

With a nod to Bree, she stepped onto the small wooden porch which circled the building, then slowly pushed the door open.

The inside of the structure was dark, the last dying strains of sunset trickling in through its sole broken window barely illuminating its interior. Its furnishings were stark and few; it looked like it had already been ransacked, likely more than once over the years since the Awakening. All that remained was a pair of rickety looking wooden chairs and a rusty metallic tub in one corner.

There was room in the middle of the cabin to place the sleeping rolls they carried in their backpacks, so they'd be able to make do. Callie unslung her pack over one shoulder and placed it on the ground.

"Hey, look, there's rainwater in this thing I think," Bree said, heading for the tub.

"Be careful, Bree, we don't know -"

Before she could finish warning her, Bree was already

too close to the tub. A dark shape rose out of it, silently looming over them both. Bree stumbled and fell backwards, scooting back toward Callie and stifling a scream.

The dark figure was once human, though how long ago no one could say. Its skin - or what remained of it - was stretched and pale, nearly translucent, even in the little light remaining. Two limbs raised up and stretched out toward them, and it opened its mouth. No sound came out, only a mouthful of black, fetid water that splatted and oozed on the wooden floor beneath it.

It was a Drowned One, unanchored and free to move.

Callie had heard whispered stories of them around the campfire. They were those who had died when the Awakened gods first returned, those who'd lived close to the sea that had given their people life, and which had ultimately cost them theirs. Since then no one dared approach the water, not unless you wanted to raise the ire of the gods.

They anchored their dead now - literally strapping heavy weights or chains to the corpses of the deceased and offering them to the Awakened Ones by throwing them in deep water. It was both a symbolic offering, meant to appease the gods, and a measure of protection for those left behind in the world of the living.

Unfortunately for them, the once-living form before them either hadn't been anchored or had somehow eluded its earthly bonds to re-emerge to the surface. As if to emphasize that point, it lifted one drenched, decomposing leg out of the tub and shuffled toward them.

It was then that the stench fully hit them, having been somewhat previously contained underwater. Callie's eyes watered, and she couldn't breathe, not until she turned her head and forced herself to inhale. She grabbed Bree by her backpack, which she hadn't removed yet, and hauled her forcefully to her feet.

"Run!" was all she could manage, not that she really had to tell Bree at that point.

The pair burst out of the structure, with Callie grabbing her own backpack on the way. The sky was a purplish black now, the colour of a deep bruise. It would've been beautiful, except for the Drowned One whose soggy footsteps could still be heard advancing upon them from inside the hut.

They first headed back the way they came, only to stop dead in their tracks. Several more creatures stood in their path now, in varying states of decay. Some had rotted lengths of rope around their waists and limbs or had rusted metallic chains dragging behind them; all of them were stretching their limbs out and inviting them into their cold embrace.

"This way!" Callie yelled, heading in the only other possible direction. Bree followed, their footsteps now splashing in the mixture of surf and sand as the water level crept up the beach.

A bone-rattling roar came from somewhere, though exactly from what or which direction Callie couldn't say. It shook her to the core, made her very bones vibrate, and the water rippled and undulated repeatedly in response.

Callie looked down into the water despite her best judgment. She swore she saw black coils of ink swirling through the stream, and she tried her best not to let the smoky tendrils touch her.

"Over there," Bree said, interrupting her train of thought. She pointed to an old wooden boat just ahead. It didn't look like the most seaworthy vessel, but they had no other options; more of the Drowned Ones floated ahead of them on the beach as well.

They veered toward the boat and strained to push it into the water. After several agonizing seconds it finally moved, and they both hopped inside of it once it was deep enough. Callie consciously avoided looking down again, though there were shapes and movement below the water in her peripheral vision just the same. She tried not to think how many more anchored yearned to grasp them from the dark depths below.

"What do we do?" asked Bree, who was looking back at the swarm of corpses amassing on the beach behind them.

They had no oars, and the water was thankfully taking them away from the shore. The further they got, the quieter the mob became, and they slowly stopped moving altogether.

"We stay quiet and wait. I think our noise attracted them, so we... we just wait." Callie didn't like that idea, but they had no other choice. She looked forward in the boat and saw a large island off on the horizon. When she squinted, it looked like a small speck of light was dancing on it.

"Is that it?" Bree asked, seeing the same light in the distance. "Callie, is that Coney?" Her eyes reflected the dim light in the distance. Hope burned within them as well, though that light was much fainter than it had ever been. Callie knew that feeling.

"Only one way to find out." It wasn't like that could go back at any rate. They were at the water's mercy now, the irony of which was not lost on her. Callie let out a bitter chuckle, then shook her head. Maybe it was a fire, or maybe it was just her imagination, but sooner or later they'd find out. For now, there was nothing either of them could do but wait.

"You get some sleep, I'll keep watch, okay?" Callie offered. The susurrus of the waves softly slapping the hull wouldn't let her sleep even if she'd wanted to do so.

While Bree arranged her knapsack into a makeshift pillow, Callie looked skyward. The stars were winking into existence, one by one, and she wondered which ones were her mother and, now, her grandmother. Whichever ones they were, she prayed they'd guide her and her sister in the right direction. She inhaled deeply, letting the salty ocean scent wash over her senses and tried to clear her mind as best she could.

She cast one last look at the receding shoreline. The Barrens, the expansive woods that had overgrown and reclaimed any and everything man-made in the last century, the only home they'd ever known, was behind them now. Ahead of them lay a different type of barrens, an angry and empty ocean.

Callie readjusted herself and stared up at the sky, searching out ancestors and answers to her questions in night sky. Both heavens and ocean remained silent.

"Look," Bree murmured, pointing up at the last pair of reddish-pink clouds clinging to the horizon. "Like cotton candy."

All Callie saw was blood.

Samuel Bauer

Samuel Bauer is a proud mathematician, Shad alumni, and part-time storyteller.

Sam's previous stories include 'The Locket,' 'Precious Pieces Unknown,' 'Dark Peaks,' 'Nucklavee,' and 'In the Rising Flame.'

He brings with him a new science-fiction tale 'Surprise Upon Landing,' as well as a reprint of his first published work, the fantasy tale 'The Locket.'

Surprise Upon Landing

The passengers on Flight 8658 settled into their cramped, unpleasant seats. Well, if they weren't unpleasant now, they would be by the time they landed, eighteen and a half hours later. It was a full flight; overbooked by about twenty-two seats. More and more jobs were moving East, people were anxious to follow them. Singapore, with its comparatively strong democracy and recent annexation of the Korean Peninsula by the Chinese made living in China a less popular option.

Tai Heng rubbed the bridge of her nose, the chatter of the passengers giving her a headache. She barely understood the ones who were speaking English. It really didn't help that English was overall the minority in terms of languages that twisted the air with their vibrations. Most people spoke either Spanish or Portuguese, and quite a few were practicing their Mandarin. Tai took up her position in the middle of the plane to give the standard safety briefing. As the tinned instructions came on over the PA, clipping painfully, Tai went through the motions, the night before still on her mind.

Bruce hung up with a satisfied sigh. He rubbed his wedding band absentmindedly, the ring a slight oval shape. As his mind turned away from his husband to the work he had to get done on the flight, he stopped rubbing the ring, instead tapping the armrest in an anxious tattoo. Then he brightened again, remembering that after this trip maybe he could finally make a social media account and not have to worry about damaging business relationships with his personal relationships. He watched out the window until the seatbelt sign turned off, then he pulled out his laptop and started to work.

In the cockpit, Kai leaned back for a moment, stretching out the kinks that had built up the night before. As his joints snapped and popped, giving him momentary relief, he turned his eyes to the radio. The comfortable, underlying murmur of radio communications was better than music, he found. He wasn't supposed to have either, but nobody really cared. Kai was careful; everyone knew that.

Tai rolled her eyes at the young men who were doing a rather bad job at hiding their stares. She knew how she looked; she didn't need some hormonal teenager's eyes to tell her that. Her smile wasn't forced. She never really had to force a smile, it was by far too practiced. That sort of simple, sympathetically cold smile, almost clinical in a way, had been so burned into her muscles that her boyfriend told her she wore it in her sleep. Correction: her ex-boyfriend.

Bruce barely felt the rumble of the engines, and he certainly didn't hear them. He had turned the music from the plane all the way up in order to be able to hear it clearly. Normally he liked to listen to the music on the plane. He had found some of his favourite bands that way. But changing the album would mean that he'd have to tear his attention away from the file that was glowing on his screen. The numbers looked wrong. He wasn't really sure why, and that pissed him off even more. Index finger tracing the somewhat ragged scar that hugged his temple, he entertained the idea that he was getting too old for this for only a moment. Then his undivided attention was back to the screen.

Kai watched his copilot absentmindedly. He was young, he guessed. He never could tell how old caucasian people were. But as more and more westerners moved east, he kept running into more and more. He could tell accents apart now. His copilot - what was his name? Herod, that was it - was a Singapore native, the slight British tinge to his words, mostly just how the t hardened. He was a good pilot; Kai liked that. A good copilot meant he could take a break. Well, for the first few hours. Eventually Herod would need to take a nap. With that thought, Kai leaned his chair back and drifted off to sleep.

Herod glanced at his sleeping copilot as if Kai had said something. He was sound asleep. Herod shook his head; the disturbance in his mind being pushed aside in favour of more immediate concerns. As he settled back into the low hum of the engines, the silence of the radio chatter went unnoticed.

Tai glanced jealously at Marie, who was curled up in the corner, not even using the full bunk. She wasn't jealous of the fact that Marie was sleeping; Tai was only two or three hours away from being able to sleep herself. She just wished she was small enough to fit on one of those bunks. But her African father had given her more than just her tone. He had also given her a height of more than six feet, almost brushing seven when she wore some modest heels. When she slept in those bunks, her body twisted up, forcing her to sleep in a way that felt like it would warp her spine irreconcilably. Marie was tiny by comparison.

They made an odd pair, pushing the refreshment trolley down the aisle, and would have made an even stranger pair in downtown Singapore if Tai didn't make sure to keep her private and professional life as far apart as possible.

Bruce rubbed the back of his neck with an agitated motion, pulling at the coarse hairs with his warm palm. It just wasn't fitting. The numbers just weren't fitting. He closed his laptop, feeling the heat radiate into his legs. Sliding open the window for the first time on the flight that was well into its fifth hour, he looked out onto the ocean. The music was still grinding at his ears, but he didn't care enough to look for something else or to check to see what ocean he was currently several hundred feet above. Instead he pulled out the ear buds and sat, watching the ocean below, the lack of clouds accentuating the vast, barren blue desert.

A rolling black cloud appeared at the horizon, spanning as far as his eyes could take it in before it sped towards the plane and vanished beyond the sight of Bruce's window. He blinked a few times, trying to recreate the illusion, but to no avail. Shrugging it off, he slid his laptop into its case, pulled out the neck pillow Simon had given him for the trip, leaned back, and fell asleep.

Tai took a moment to rest her legs. Most of the flight was asleep, and her left calf was killing her. It seemed to pound in a syncopated beat, out of time with her heartbeat. She reached down, sliding up her pants leg and feeling the smooth skin of her tattoo. Her fingertips traced the outline of the snake that was coiled there. She reached up, grabbing a tea towel and a handful of the ice. After about a half hour of holding the frigid packet against her tattoo, she felt good enough to get up. Dumping the rest of the ice into the sink, she pulled the trolley with all of the pillows and blankets out of the closet, and started pushing it down the hallway, not feeling the blood that started to leak out of the five year old tattoo.

Kai rubbed the sleep from his eyes. Herod blinked slowly, shutting his eyes for a little bit too long. Kai gave him a friendly tap on the shoulder. Herod nodded, and laid back in his chair. In a few moments he was asleep. Kai fiddled with the radio for a moment to try to get the low buzz of voices back, but there was nothing. He shrugged; there might have been an issue with the receiver on his end, but if there was, the system hadn't seen it yet. Or it was probably just an issue with the satellites. Ever since the Americans had broken the Outer Space Treaty in the 2020's, there had been more and more blackouts as unrestricted satellite warfare had truly begun between the Americans and the Chinese. Of course, neither party had so much as said as much, but it was pretty obvious.

Still, just to be sure, Kai ran a diagnostic. He was all clear; must be an issue on their end. He just hoped that it was all resolved by the time he got to Singapore. In - he glanced at the clock - five hours.

He'd landed a plane in much worse though.

There was a knock at the door that interrupted his train of thought. He called, not so much making words as some basal noise, for whoever it was to come in. A stewardess came in and wordlessly set out his breakfast. He nodded his thanks, and turned back to the controls while sipping on his coffee.

Bruce watched the sea below dip and curve almost imperceptibly. The waters seemed to form words in some arcane script in Bruce's imagination. He shifted uncomfortably in his seat. He indicated to the woman sitting next to him that he would like to get out into the aisle. He squeezed past her, and made his way to the bathroom.

He splashed the lukewarm water on his face, and shook his hands dry. There was a moment of looking at himself in the mirror before he turned and threw up black bile, almost missing the toilet. He dropped to his knees, feeling his stomach twist and turn and convulse.

Tai watched as the whole plane seemed to empty their stomachs in eerie unison.

Fortunately for them, most of the passengers had the foresight to grab the sick bags. She felt her stomach turn, but held it back long enough to get out of sight of the passengers and throw up into the trash. After a minute of dry heaving, she stood back up, wiped her mouth with a napkin, and pivoted to go help the passengers.

People were looking into the sick bags with a puzzled look on their faces. Tai looked over one of their shoulders to see an empty bag.

She shrugged, and turned around to go get some sleep in the cramped bed. She must be seeing things again.

Kai shook Herod awake. He blinked slowly, confusedly looking at Kai. Kai pointed out the front window.

Flying in front of the plane were several creatures unlike anything they had ever seen outside of some books.

They were massive animals, with wingspans of several meters, long beaks, and iridescent colours.

They were pterodactyls. They dove down, pulling away from the passenger plane like fighter jets, and disappeared. The two men looked at each other, and decided that the remaining half an hour to Singapore would have two pilots.

Bruce returned to his seat, and pulled on his seatbelt. The woman sitting next to him shook her head.

Must have been a bad meal. Must have.
Are you sure? Everyone had it.
What else could it be?
It was a rough landing, and the radio was silent.
They slid down the emergency slide.
Everyone stood on the tarmac in shock.
Singapore burned.
Strange creatures flew through the air.

Tai was the first to speak.
"What the--"

The Lockett

An excerpt from the files of St. Dymphna Hospital for the Mentally Ill (1845-1896), published for the interest of the public.

Found written on the back of R. Cole's patient file sheet:

What I have to say concerning the late Mr. Theodore Loft is unusual in the extreme, and as such, has no suitable space on our standard forms. Mr. Loft arrived to us from the nearby HMQ Mental Hospital, owing to the fact that the psychiatric ward there was overflowing, and Mr. Loft had no known next of kin or associates.

As noted on the patient file sheet, Mr. Loft suffered from hallucinations. These hallucinations were distressing in the extreme, and resulted in regular, but not frequent, violent and self-damaging outbursts. He would attempt to end the hallucinations by damaging his eyes or ears, and attack anybody nearby who attempted to stop him. Preceding these episodes, he would mumble incoherently about a "Matilda," apologizing and acting as if she was conversing with him. He would ignore any stimuli, other than to resist the nurses attempting to restrain him from self-harm. After a short period of about thirty seconds, he would then attempt to gouge out his own eyes, or become extremely violent towards the nurses. Immediately upon recovering, he would fall into a fitful sleep.

In the three months that he was here, he had twelve outbursts, and severely injured two nurses, Mrs. Holloway and my wife, Joan. Mrs. Holloway has since recovered and now is working with more peaceful patents. Upon discovering that he had injured Mrs. Holloway, Mr. Loft came to my office and asked if he was still allowed to stay, as he had grown to love the south gardens that he tended. I told him of course he was allowed to stay, and he could stay until he was ready to leave. One month later, he injured Joan. This time, I was the one who was there when he woke up. He was mortified, and I reassured him that he could stay. The next outburst, his heart was put under so much pressure that he died.

I had conversed with the man, in hopes of finding out what tortured him. He was reluctant to tell me what it was exactly, but he told me of how he was a simple farmhand, living in barns and working for food and lodgings. Whenever he was asked if he had a lover, he would fall silent and taciturn, and he would refuse any and all advances. He had few possessions when he came to the hospital, but his most prized was a locket around his neck. He never removed it except for sleeping and bathing, but even then he would not let it out of his sight. I never saw him look into it, but he was protective of it, and would not let anyone touch it.

After his death, I went through his possessions and found a will. It stated that he donated all of his possessions to the hospital, but that the locket must be buried with him. I looked through his possessions, and upon finding the small locket, I peered inside. I now wish that I had not.

As I opened it, I experienced a vision that filled my senses. The stench of burnt flesh tore at my nostrils, and I saw my wife Joan burning alive in a flame. Her pained screams tore at my ears. When I came to, I was in a cold sweat on the floor. The locket lay before me, opened. Engraved inside was D.F. I closed the foul thing, and buried it with the man. The terrible vision I hoped was buried with him. But some things cannot be sealed by mere earth.

Two months later, Joan and I moved to a small cottage just off of the grounds. My disposition had grown more nervous, and she felt that being away from the patients might alleviate my stress. On the third day, I returned home to my wife from the hospital, as she had taken ill recently and was nauseas, and as such, was staying at home resting. As I approached my house, a smell of smoke filled the air. My mouth grew dry as I recalled that terrible vision. As I began to run, the house became engulfed in flames.

The first thing I heard was the screams. Horror engulfed my mind, charring away any rational thought. I rushed inside and found my wife in the kitchen, passed out. I ran from the house. I laid her gently on the ground. I used my bare hands to put out the flames that covered her dress. I felt her wrist. There was no pulse. Desperate, I did what one should use to save a person who has drowned. I breathed into her nostril, and then applied pressure to her chest. I continued to simulate natural breathing, but all was in vain. She had perished.

I now write these words with scarred hands. The flames that stole my wife burned my body as well as my heart. When I walk these halls, often I hear her voice echoing back at me, unintelligibly. I hear the screams of newborns, though our hospital has no place for children. And sometimes, I can see her face, burnt and red, staring at me, with pleading eyes. And now, in the dead of night as I write these words, I can hear her footsteps coming nearer. She is calling out to me. Pleading as to why I could not save her. And my mouth is numb. I cannot speak, only mumble. Mumble out the words:

Joan, I'm sorry.

Dr. Rufus Cole, PHD.

Chantal Boudreau

A Toronto native currently living in Sambro, Nova Scotia, Boudreau is an avid and prolific author with over sixty credits to her name. She is the author of the Fervor series of novels, as well as the *Masters & Renegades* series and *The Snowy Barrens* Trilogy.

Boudreau is likely best known for her work in short fiction, and the anthologies she has appeared in have been shortlisted for both the Bram Stoker award and the Aurora award.

Her extensive short-fiction bibliography includes fantasy, dark fantasy, and horror.

She brings with her reprints of her tales from *Chillers from the Rock* and *Dystopia from the Rock*, respectively.

Territory

Samantha Cook had been a realtor for much of her adult life, and was one of the better salespeople at her realty firm. That was why she had been assigned the Berman Street house. The house had gone through five owners in the last three years, and was now recognized in her firm as a "problem property." Considered a hard sell, management had made the executive decision to add it to Samantha's portfolio. They believed only a few of their realtors were capable of unloading it for a fifth time. Samantha happened to be one of those realtors.

Not that there was anything physically wrong with the house. The building was in fine form, and it came with a reasonably sized and well-tended estate. Inspectors could find nothing wrong with the place, and as long as a potential customer didn't know the house's history, Samantha had no problem seeding their interest, especially with an unusually low asking price. The problem was that Windsor had a small town mentality and that meant that everyone knew everybody else's business. Rumours had already infiltrated the community as to why new owners were so quick to abandon the place. As a result, Samantha could only hope for a sale involving an outsider. Nobody local was even willing to go anywhere near the place, let alone take ownership.

Samantha glanced over at the file folder on the passenger seat. Fortunately, her next potential buyer was such an outsider – a single woman, a divorcee actually, from a neighbouring area. Samantha liked divorcees. They often had the urgent desire to change their surroundings and compromised much more quickly than the average married soul -- anything to escape a place haunted by memories.

Haunted -- Samantha chided herself for thinking the word. She didn't want to jinx this sale from the get-go.

Her cell phone rang.

"Allen's Realty. Samantha speaking."

"Heeeey, Cookie. She run off screaming yet?" The voice on the other end belonged to Scott, a rival realtor at her firm. He had phoned to taunt Samantha, a little disgruntled that management had chosen her to handle the Berman Street challenge over him, but also somewhat relieved that it was her problem and not his.

"I'm still waiting for her to get here, Scott. Now bugger off. I don't want your kind of bad luck to rub off on me. I've got a good feeling about this one. As long as she doesn't get wind of what the previous owners believed they saw, I think she may be a sure thing."

"Bah! No such thing. Not that it matters, and no extra pressure, but we've got a betting pool going at the office. I say she bolts." Scott sounded cocky.

Samantha knew better than to play these games with Scott. This was his method of trash talking her, trying to throw her off in hopes that she would fail and, in the process, make him look better. She wasn't about to let him spoil a positive vibe, so she decided it was time to get rid of him.

"Oh, look at that. She's driving up now. Got to go, Scott. It's time to work my magic."

Samantha hung up without giving a chance to answer. She had no compunctions about lying to him. Stretching the truth was a big part of her job – the trick was in not going far enough to cause a fraud lawsuit. The Berman Street property was going to require some expert exaggeration and adept omission of fact. Considering that the prior owners' issues with the house could not be scientifically proven made the latter fairly simple. Nobody could accuse Samantha of failing to disclose something that didn't legitimately exist.

Samantha glanced at her watch, aware that time was of the essence. The potential buyer, a woman by the name of Natalie Raymond, was already a few minutes late. Much longer, and the delay would throw off Samantha's entire schedule for the day. With an impatient sigh, she slung her purse over her shoulder and stepped out of the car.

The well-primped woman stood, straightening her company-standard blazer before approaching the front of the house. Her high heels clacked against the pavement as she hurried up the paved driveway. Once standing in front of the door, hands on hips, she eyed it as if facing down an opponent on the battlefield.

"If you give me a hard time on this sale, I'm bringing in an exorcist – I swear. You behave or else," Samantha threatened.

The house didn't respond in any way, but it felt to Samantha as if the building were returning her stare with eerie resistance. She just may have a fight on her hands after all. However, this house, from all accounts, was a bully and bullies were essentially cowards. Samantha didn't get where she was by being a pushover or by backing down, especially not in the face of a bully. While not worried about her own ability to cope with the unruly property, her concern was the nature of her client. All she needed was for the presence in the house to keep quiet until the showing was done.

Drawing her from her confrontation, the sound of gravel crunching between tires and pavement caught Samantha's attention and she turned to see a car pulling up behind her own. A woman, probably in her early thirties, emerged looking harried and in a foul mood. She tossed a cigarette butt onto the shoulder of the road and ground it into the dirt with her heel.

The newcomer wore dishevelled clothing, as if she had dressed in a rush, and her hair, pulled back in a haphazard ponytail, escaped in small wisps in places, fluttering around her head in the slight breeze that brushed past her. The most unpleasant part of her appearance was her facial expression. Samantha had never had a client arrive at a viewing with such a terrible scowl on their face. She noted that this would add an extra level of difficulty to an already challenging situation. It was always a struggle to get someone with a negative attitude to see a property in a positive light.

"Ms. Raymond?" Samantha asked with a bright smile, extending her hand in greeting.

Very careful about how she addressed her clients, she was always professional, never calling anyone by their first name unless invited to do so, and never addressing a divorcee as either Mrs. or Miss. They were quick to take offense, their marital status often a touchy subject.

The client ignored the gesture. She nodded in response, pushing the loose hair away from her face as she glared at the house.

"Don't call me that. It just reminds me I've been too busy to get my name legally changed back to my maiden name. Call me Natalie. And don't waste any small talk on me. Just show me the house and tell me what you can about it."

Samantha was taken aback. Natalie offered none of the pleasantries one might expect upon meeting someone for the first time, and no apologies for arriving late. She had a harshness to her, rough around the edges, that Samantha had certainly not been expecting. From the client's file, based on her financial information, she was well educated and decently employed, so Samantha had been anticipating a certain level of social etiquette. She had to wonder if Natalie's demeanour was all the result of her involvement in a bitter divorce, or if there were something more to it.

Natalie gave her a dissatisfied look.

"Well, are we going to stand here all day, or are we going in?"

"Of course, of course," Samantha acquiesced, her tone apologetic. "Please, follow me."

She led Natalie into the foyer and turned on the light there, although it was mostly unnecessary. The house had plenty of southern facing windows and the foyer was bathed in sunlight.

"It's big and bright," the unhappy woman remarked. "I was hoping for something smaller... and less friendly. I would have expected it at the asking price."

"It is large for one person," Samantha agreed as she swept into the next room. "But that presents the opportunity for boarders. With that as a means of income, this house could practically pay for itself. What a wonderful investment!"

"I don't work well with boarders," was Natalie's sullen response. "I have every intention of living alone. I need peace and quiet for a change."

Samantha wondered if this had anything to do with some sort of tumultuous relationship with her ex-husband. The file had indicated that Natalie had no children. Based on the woman's temperament, Samantha doubted she had much in the way of friends either.

"Well, there is plenty of space between you and any neighbour, so they certainly won't be bothering you, and there is very little traffic on this street. I suspect you would get an abundance of peace and quiet here, if that's what you're looking for."

"That's not what I meant," Natalie told her, but she did not elaborate further. Samantha knew better than to pry.

The realtor noted that Natalie was unusually quiet as she toured the house, barely glancing at any of the preferred features pointed out to her. That didn't bode well for a sale; a truly interested potential buyer always asked questions. Experience told Samantha that much.

It wasn't until they arrived at the final room, one of the smaller bedrooms upstairs intended for a child, that Natalie broke her silence. The room also happened to be the one Samantha dreaded showing the most. If there was going to be trouble, it would likely happen there. After a quick once over, Samantha was ready to usher her out. Natalie stood her ground, however, and posed her first question.

"So what can you tell me about the ghost that lives here?"

Aghast, Samantha searched her mind for a way of answering that without assuring the loss of a sale. She had been hoping this out-of-towner would have no idea why the prior owners had left the place in such a hurry, willing to forego a sale price that matched what they had paid, just to be rid of the house. Until that moment, Samantha had considered herself fortunate. While they had walked the circuit of the rooms, there had been no phantom sounds, no transparent visions, and no upsets of any of the staging decor. She had considered herself spared of any such nuisances, ones that would require explanation.

Samantha gave Natalie a nervous smile. "What, the old rumours and wives' tales suggesting this place is haunted? Those are just spread by the locals to scare off outsiders. Everyone knows ghosts don't exist. There's no point to those stories."

Natalie's expression hardened, something Samantha thought wasn't possible.

"Humour me," she said.

Her worst fears realized, Samantha resigned herself to considering this showing a lost cause. She took a seat in one of the chairs that had been used to stage the room. This would probably take some time, and her feet ached after rounding the house in particularly uncomfortable heels.

"Alright, I can give you an abridged version of the tall-tale I have heard. Apparently, this home once belonged to a local couple who had a couple of sons. The eldest, a boy by the name of Alvin, was reputed to be a bit of a town bully. In particular, he considered this house and the surrounding area his 'territory' and any other child he caught passing through here, he would charge a toll. If they didn't pay, he beat them up. Apparently one day, one of his victims snapped, and decided he wasn't going to take it anymore. He stashed a weapon in his pack, a knife, so he could defend himself against Alvin's bullying. When Alvin jumped this child, the smaller boy fought back with the knife, stabbing Alvin and killing him. The stories claim that Alvin has never left here. He still haunts his 'territory', roaming the house, yard, and street to torment those who haven't paid his toll. They say he's even meaner now that he's dead – that he's still angry at the kid who killed him. He haunts children more so than adults."

Samantha hoped this last fact might lessen the blow, since Natalie had no children of her own.

Natalie stood there, so placid and exceptionally quiet that poor Samantha found it horribly unnerving. Although she had given the potential buyer only half of the story, the realtor knew the tale well. The last family who lived in the house had deserted the place after their youngest child had been hospitalized when a heavy vase had launched itself off of the mantelpiece of the living room fireplace striking the girl in the head and knocking her unconscious. No one could claim that it had merely fallen on her after it had toppled by chance, since the girl had been more than a metre away when it had happened.

That had been the last straw for the parents, having already been subject to a series of similar occurrences, escalating in severity. They had moved out later that week, putting the house on the market at a price that allowed for as big a loss as they could afford to take -- anything to be rid of it.

Waiting for such a long time for a response from Natalie made Samantha uncomfortable. She gave a nervous little laugh before speaking. "Of course, the rumours are just that, a way for local folks to scare away outsiders. They're not all that fond of strangers, but they do warm up to you once you've been here for a little while. It really is a nice neighbourhood once you've settled in."

The air in the room seemed to chill as quickly as the look in Natalie's icy blue eyes. She crossed her arms and pursed her lips.

"That's a pity," she said. "I was counting on the stories proving to be true. I guess I'll have to keep looking."

This statement confused Samantha. She couldn't fathom the idea that someone would actually want a house that was haunted, specifically because there was a ghost present. It didn't make any sense.

Before she could wrap her head around the notion, she was forced to change her train of thought abruptly. If she hadn't redirected her attention, she wouldn't have managed to duck in time to avoid the die-cast metal airplane that was suddenly winging its way at her head. Samantha barely avoided being struck by the nasty projectile, which instead crashed into the wall behind her.

Natalie smiled for the first time since Samantha had met her, an expression that bore an air of the Machiavellian.

"Never mind," she said. "I'll take it."

Natalie pulled the last box from her car and rested against the vehicle's cold, hard metal surface. She would find a place to stash the box along with the others, but she wouldn't be unpacking right away. She had some preparations to make first, ones she hoped would cure her of her greatest blight.

"This isn't home. I need to go home. You have to tell them the truth. You have to set me free." The disembodied voice that echoed around Natalie's head had the pitch of a small child.

"Shut up, Annette. This is my home now. If you don't like it, get lost. You know you're not welcome to hang around with me. You never were and you never will be." *That's why I'm in this mess,* Natalie thought. "You ruined my life, you ruined my marriage, and I'll be happy to be rid of you after all of these years."

She hoisted the box up onto her shoulder and lugged her tired body up the front steps. When she opened the door, she made sure to give warning, glancing around the empty foyer.

"This is the last of my stuff, Alvin. I have your toll and I intend to pay it. Let me just put this down and I'll go get it from the car. I think we're going to be friends, you and I. I'm willing to play by your rules." Natalie spoke out loud, even though she appeared to be alone. She didn't wait for a reply. Once fully inside the house, she haphazardly shoved the box she carried into a random corner, before heading back towards her car.

More words from nowhere: *"It's all your fault, Nattie. All you have to do is tell them. Confess, and I'll leave you alone."*

"I've told you a million times, Annette. You can't be my conscience and I don't have one of my own. You are wasting your time and mine. This is your last warning. Go away, or suffer the consequences," Natalie said. She pulled a cigarette from her purse and lit it before grabbing the plastic bag that rested on her passenger seat.

Preparation – it was all about preparation. In fact, this was the last stage of her preparation. Natalie had begun with a search for a house reputed to be haunted, and then she had done her research. This house had held the most promise for what she had in mind. Once she had assured herself that the story wasn't a hoax, Natalie had dug a little deeper. A trip to the local tavern where she made herself friendly by buying a round of drinks had yielded results. She had managed to locate Stanley, the great uncle of the legendary Alvin, and a few more drinks had netted Natalie the tale in its entirety, with all the gory details. Uncle Stanley had been even willing to tell her everything he happened to know about Alvin, once the alcohol had loosened his tongue. He admitted his nephew, Alvin's father, had been a bully as well and had beaten both his sons on a regular basis. It was likely why Alvin had taken to bullying in turn, a transferral of his rage to someone weaker than himself

The discussion with Uncle Stanley had led to another revelation. The answer to her problem of how to cope with Alvin was jellybeans. That had been Alvin's favourite treat, Uncle Stanley had told her. Natalie realized that a phantom child couldn't eat candy, but it was the offering that counted, not the consumption. She gave the bag in her hand a shake as she started up the front step. The rattle of the candies within brought a smile to her face.

"What are you doing, Nattie? Home, I want to go home. Let me rest. Tell them. Tell them the truth."

"Mind your own business, Annette," Natalie said between puffs on her cigarette.

She paused long enough to dig a bowl out of one of the boxes labelled "kitchen" and started up the stairs, bag in one hand, bowl in the other, and cigarette held between clenched teeth. Once she had arrived in the room where the toy plane had almost taken the realtor's head off, she placed the bowl in the middle of the room and filled it with jellybeans. She addressed the room in general.

"These are for you, Alvin. I'm paying your toll, so that you leave me in peace. I'll check the bowl daily, and if you need a refill, consider it done. But I want this to be especially clear – this toll is for me and only for me. It doesn't cover anyone else who happens to be trespassing into your territory, and you may have noticed that I didn't come here alone."

"Nattie – why are you doing this? You set this up on purpose," the ghostly voice whispered. *"This isn't fair."*

"Neither is haunting me for fifteen years, you little witch," Natalie snarled, sealing the bag with the jellybeans. "I don't know how many more times I have to tell you. It was an accident! – An accident!"

She stood up, slinging the bag over her shoulder and flicking ash off of her cigarette.

"Do you want to know who else is here, intruding in your territory, Alvin? This is my little sister, Annette. The little brat used to follow me everywhere. Just like now, she wouldn't leave me alone. I told her I would give her trouble then, but she wouldn't listen anymore than she does today. Well, she's going to pay for that now. You hear that, Annette?"

Natalie's voice reverberated around the mostly empty room. This time there was no response.

"Oh, so now you get quiet on me. Do you want to know how it all went down, Alvin? I told Little-Miss-Tag-Along not to follow me, as per usual. I was going to meet a boy – one I wasn't supposed to see because he had a bad reputation. I was meeting him in the park, but I had to walk the long trail along the ravine. She walked up behind me while I was on my way, and said that she knew who I was meeting and that she was going to rat me out. I told her to get lost and I gave her a shove. I wasn't trying to make her fall, just push her back. But she rolled down the side of the ravine and hit her head on a rotting log.

When I went to check on her, she was already dead, so I just left her there. I pretended like I didn't know where she had gone when she didn't come home by nightfall. It was no big deal; a man walking his dog found her three days later."

The jellybeans rattled in the bowl. Natalie took that as a sign that Alvin was paying attention.

"I'm sure you know what I mean, Alvin," she continued. "You were a big brother once. You probably remember how much of a pest your younger brother was. The whole thing was her fault. She shouldn't have been following me. She shouldn't have harassed me. But then, Annette kept haranguing me, long after death, probably the most persistent of pests. She said I had to confess so she could rest, but I didn't kill her on purpose so I'm not about to confess to a murder I didn't commit. It's not like what happened with you. That little boy brought that knife planning to use it on you. He was most definitely guilty."

Natalie had no intention of mentioning the fact that Alvin's killer considered it self-defence. She wanted to rile the phantom bully up as much as possible, but convince him that she, personally, was on his side. She was also hoping to generate some sympathy towards her own situation. She allowed her shoulders to sag and gently nudged the jellybean bowl with her foot.

"I'm tired, Alvin. I'm really tired. Day and night, I have to put up with her, and her nonsense. She thinks she's better than me and she hardly ever shuts up. She's driving me crazy. I barely made it through school, but I had an easier time ignoring her then and I resorted to drugs to get me through the worst of it. Her constant pestering destroyed my marriage – sex sucks when you have a voice hounding you about how she wants to go home the entire time – and now it's even threatening my job. When she forced me to go on stress leave, I realized that I was going to have to take some desperate measures. That's why I'm here, Alvin. That's why I'm paying the toll... just for me, not for her. I just need a little peace, after all these years."

That was when the noises began. The room started shaking, windows and jellybean bowl rattling like there was a minor earthquake. The swirling winds within the room and the howling followed, guttural sounds of rage and whimpering noises, as if a battle had commenced within those walls. But it wasn't an even fight. Odds definitely fell in favour of the violent bully, enraged that another had invaded his territory without paying the toll, and taking out years of frustration on the lost soul that had accompanied Natalie as she had moved into the house.

Despite the chaotic struggle that she left within the room, Natalie wore a large smile as she stepped into the hallway and closed the door behind her. Perhaps Annette was right. Perhaps in her heart of hearts she had been trying to hurt the girl that day alongside the ravine, but she'd never admit to it. The way she figured, Natalie had done her penance: fifteen years of torment and suffering seemed like a reasonable sentence for her crime. She now had a refuge and all it required was remaining in Alvin's territory and paying his toll – like transitioning to a halfway house. Natalie could handle that.

The noise wasn't all that bad the farther away she moved from the room, and in the farthest reaches of the house, the shaking could only be felt as a mild tremor. Once she was far away within the house as she could get, Natalie pulled a book out of one of her boxes and sank happily into a chair. She relaxed, wearing an expression of pure bliss.

"Ahhh," she sighed. "Peace at last."

Cash Grab

"I'm here. Cutting it close, but the VP called me into his office to go over strategic initiatives. I got back as quickly as I could."

Jessie strode into the interview room, joining the remainder of the interview panel. She looked uncomfortable in her pantsuit and heels which, at an Amazonian 5'11", seemed like an unnecessary addition. The way her suit clung to her suggested it belonged on a woman of different proportions, bunching over her back, shoulders, hips, and thighs.

"You can't say no to Buck," Owen said.

The faux leather of his chair creaked, accommodating his girth. Bearing a few gray hairs and wrinkles, he was almost as broad as he was tall -- the football team captain long after high school. Unlike Jessie, he seemed at ease in his dress shirt and tie, despite his bulging biceps.

Art, on the other side, offered contrast. His form long and lean, he had the weary but athletic appearance of a marathon runner.

"Now that we have our full interview panel, let's call the first candidate."

Art hopped from his chair and left the room. Jessie poured herself a glass of water, sweat beading on her forehead.

"Looks like Buck ran you through the ringer," Owen remarked, eying her dishevelled black hair.

"You don't know the half of it. He's worried about replacing Murray so close to budget sessions. He wants a cohesive team, but there's hardly time for training."

"He was having hip troubles and issues with his knees. Old age gets us all in the end. We'll be handicapped having a newbie, but they'll have youth and enthusiasm going for them. Hopefully, we'll find someone longterm."

"I hear Natural Resources is offering a signing bonus for a service agreement," Jessie said.

Owen rolled his eyes. "That's because they have wiggle room. They're not stretched thin like us. Even if they don't rate top numbers, they don't have the financial demands we do."

Art reappeared at the door. "They'll be along in a couple of minutes. Are you going on about Natural Resources again?"

"A department that small shouldn't have that good a budgeting team," Owen insisted. "If we don't make the numbers work, people can die."

"On a brighter note -- Education just lost its star player." Jessie took another swig from her water.

Art swung back into his chair. "Annika? Really?"

Jessie nodded. "Pregnant."

"I thought she was one of those dedicated career women?"

"Rumour says it was a one-night stand and she's a pro-lifer. She's out for now -- maybe for good."

"I can't say I'm sorry. Education's our biggest opponent," Owen said. "With her out of the way, we'll have a better chance, even with a rookie."

"Not necessarily a rookie." Art pointed at the papers before him. "Did you see this guy's resume? Ivy league, lots of extra-curriculars. Spent time in Community Services' finance section. It might be nice having an addition with budgeting experience."

A soft knock on the door made him pause. Marley, their receptionist, glanced in. "I have Mr. Lockhart. Are you ready?"

They nodded. A man wandered in, medium height and older, a little on the thin side, balding on top, but he carried himself with confidence and offered a strong handshake. They made their introductions and started in with their questions.

Mr. Lockhart offered quick and thorough responses, asking appropriate questions himself. He clearly knew everything to know about finance.

As Art showed him out, Jessie chewed the end of her pen, while Owen gripped his chair. Once they were out of earshot, Owen groaned.

"He can't be serious. He couldn't hold his own in a department like ours."

"He apparently managed to pass the stress test. That's all they need to avoid being screened out. HR always lets a couple like him through." Jessie gestured at the papers with her pen. "Art missed something. The resume says budgeting 'sub-committee'. He's never played in the big leagues."

"Why do these guys who've made their careers in the minor leagues expect to come here now? He never had what it took to make the cut when he was younger. He's past his prime."

Jessie leaned in. "Who's next on deck?"

"Pamela Wallace -- some woman just out of the accounting program at the local college. I won't be holding my breath."

"It says she did track and field in high school." Jessie waved the resume at Owen.

Art returned, shaking his head.

"He was no Murray -- heck, Ruben at Environment could have given him the business and he's only there because he's the director's son."

After a quiet knock on the door, Marley peered in. "Are you ready for Ms. Wallace?"

"Sure," Owen replied.

The young woman who walked in and took a seat was almost as broad as Owen and taller than Jessie. Jessie flashed the newcomer a smile, offering her hand. "You did track and field? What was your sport?"

"Sports," Pamela stated. Jessie cringed from the firmness of her grip. "Shotput and hammer-throw. Our team place first in our division."

"You don't say." Owen gave his panel peers his best "we have a winner" look.

"There's not much call for track and field pros and coaching pays a pittance compared to government jobs, so my dad told me to take accounting. He said it would be the best way to get my foot in the door. I'm not big on the number-crunching, but I like the idea of being on the budgeting team."

They ran through the required financial questions, making it clear this was primarily for ceremony. They could easily fudge the grading to put her through if she grasped simple things like addition and subtraction, and she knew which end of a calculator was up.

By the time Pamela left, a heightened energy had formed in the room. When the door closed behind her,

Art abandoned his serious expression for one thoroughly giddy.

"Screw Murray. If we can replace him with her, I'm glad he's gone."

Jessie eyed the closed door with a sigh. "I just hope we can keep her. We'll have her for this round of budgeting, but if she puts in a good performance this year, everybody and their dog will be offering her some sort of secondment."

Owen nodded before dropping the remaining folder of resumes and empty interview booklets into the paper shredder.

There was no point in going any further -- they had their debut star.

"Pam -- hey, Pam! Over here."

Jessie waved her cohort over. She eyed Pam with admiration.

"Wow -- the new uniform suits you."

While not required to wear suits and ties to budget meetings, the dress code did call for "business casual." In the past, that had meant scratchy golf shirts with roomy cargo pants. They always had trouble finding ones big enough to fit Owen in a way that didn't restrict his movement.

Their work wear had changed this year. In addition to adding star power to their team, Pam had suggested a new uniform. Fine-ance Gear, a trendy upstart, was happy to donate some of their stretch-wear business casual line in exchange for openly displaying their product logos. The stylish clothing had surprising give, despite not looking in any way like activewear. Even Owen looked comfortable.

"What's the plan?" Pam asked.

"First round's a shoo-in, top-tier versus bottom-tier. I looked up the roster and we're up against Culture and Heritage. They've bottomed out three years running. It sucks for the museums, but it works for us. They hardly have enough to pay for washouts. They've had 100% staff turnover since the budget sessions last year," Art told her.

"They look okay to me."

Art laughed.

"Looks can be deceptive. Joy over there refuses to participate without heels -- she's more concerned with image than results."

"I've heard she gets hefty endorsements from shoe companies, so she doesn't care about the government paying her a pittance," Jessie added.

"Along with that major handicap, they have Betty." Art pointed at a wiry-looking, wrinkled woman with silver hair.

"Seriously? She looks like she's a hundred."

"Not quite, but she refuses to retire. She was reasonably sharp for the skill-testing questions right up until last year, when she took a blow to the head during a skirmish. Now she mixes up some of the policies and her hands have a permanent tremor. They can't oust her because she's union, so she keeps getting traded around the bottom-tier teams."

"Sad," Pam said. "I hope I know when it's my time to bow out. What about him?" She gestured towards a man with a physique similar to Art's, his eyes a little yellow.

"Frank? Frank's an alcoholic crap shoot. If they kept him sober for the last couple of months, he'll be fine. If the stress got to him and he hit the bottle, they can't expect much."

"I heard opposing bottom-tiered teams have purposely sabotaged Frank in the past. It's dirty pool, but there's nothing preventing it," Jessie added.

"What about him?" Pam pointed at their last team member, a slightly thinner version of Owen.

Art shook his head. "Peter was one of the good ones before he threw out his back. He should have stepped down to the subcommittees three years ago. If he doesn't perform this year, he'll end up there anyway. Some people can't accept change."

"Come on." Jessie grabbed Art by the arm. "Flag's up. They're ready for us."

"What's going on?" Pam asked Owen as their two cohorts headed off.

"You have to show a minimal level of finance competency before you can move on to the physical competition. If you don't, you default-- Oh no -- really?"

Pam glanced at the opponent's table. "What?"

"They sent in Joy and Betty. Joy's a low performer, but she can muddle through. She won't do well enough to make up for an underperformer like Betty. Frank must be drunk or hungover."

"What about Peter?"

Owen chuckled. "He's a ringer, like me, or at least he was. We're not number-crunchers. We're here for brute force."

Pam gave him an uncomfortable look, realizing she might be one too.

"Don't worry," he said. "We won't last as long, but we get better promotions -- including hefty retirement plans. Plus, we have great disability coverage. We're more likely to get endorsements too."

"Can I ask why budgeting's done this way? It used to be different."

"You get one reality star interfering in government and the next thing you know, everyone wants a piece of it. We had a particularly mercenary government in place when the changes were made. They decided the way to increase coffers without increasing taxes was to make what we do interesting to the public. Turn it into entertainment and suddenly we have plenty more money to work with. So that's what they did. They took their governing majority and set us up as reality TV with a dose of pro-sports mixed in. Add some wealthy sponsors and boom -- no more deficits. Even in the years we flubbed the cash grab, we still had more to work with than the times we had to rely solely on taxes. Everyone's better off."

Pam watched poor Betty, moaning and pulling at her hair, clearly having some sort of emotional meltdown as she struggled with the questions before her. "Are we -- really?"

Owen shrugged. "Sure, there will be Bettys, but there are people who suffer as a result of any system. Give the people what they want so we can give them what they need -- that's the new world order's motto."

"People don't need culture and heritage?"

"It's not just department size that decides the quality of the budgeting team. If the public values the team, they can choose to make a political donation to sponsor a good trade or a lucrative signing bonus. If the dollars don't roll in, it's because people don't care."

Pam wasn't so sure about that. She had heard rumors of kickbacks, Big Pharma sponsoring Health in order to be given preferential treatment during RFPs and supplier contract agreements, and Natural Resources handed donations by Big Oil and mining companies for the same reason. Meanwhile, the smaller departments or those with little to offer businesses, ignored by corporations, languished during the budget sessions. Now she was seeing an example of this first hand.

The bell rang to indicate time was up. After a quick review, the ref checking Health's answers lifted a hand -- a sign of success. The other ref shook his head. Team Culture and Heritage had failed the prelims.

"At least if Betty doesn't retire after this, they'll have a good excuse to dump her into a sub-committee."

Pam's expression fell. Not only did she feel sorry for Betty, but she also had been anticipating whatever physical component lay ahead of them. Now it would just be more waiting.

Owen patted her shoulder. "Cheer up -- we get a free pass. We can save our energy and avoid risking injury competing against a bottom tier. Better to go in fresh against a mid-tier or top-tier team. We definitely don't want to start the year working with a loser's budget."

Owen's expression could only be described as glum returning from the board posting the second level roster.

"Let me guess," Jessie said. "Natural Resources?"

Owen hung his head.

"Default in round one, and they pit you against a top mid-tier in round two. It's the way it works." Art tilted his head, eying the other budget team sideways. "The endorsements are numerous. I count two oil companies, one mining company, and a solar panel manufacturer. Their gear looks better than ours."

Jessie strained her neck and squinted, looking for the manufacturer's mark. "Mmmm, Aiken's Competitive Gold Line. I heard they branched into budgeting wear. Those aren't freebies for product promotion -- not an endorsement deal either. The manufacturer's mark isn't visible enough. They paid through the nose for those."

"They get to pick the physical challenge because they're the lower ranking team." Owen groaned. "They're a bunch of lightweights and they're going to pick speed over strength."

"I guess it's a good thing I'm fast," Pam said.

"We'll be counting on you and our wonder woman, Jessie. Art's our endurance man. He's a slower burn but he can hold out forever."

Art went to fetch the challenge call.

"Start stretching," Jessie advised.

"Don't we still have the skill-testing questions?" Pam asked.

"Nope -- that's just a first round formality. Once you qualify, you're good. We'll be starting shortly."

Art was grimacing upon his return.

Pam didn't like that expression. "What did they call?"

"Fiduciary Freak-out."

Relieved that it wasn't one of her weaker challenges, Pam realized Owen had been right. Freak-out was a high-paced game Jessie had described as "interoffice rugby with makeshift weapons." They had to run a cubicle maze trying to score on their opponents' goal, while preventing their opponent from scoring in turn. You had to be fast and plays were over quickly.

"Okay, Jess, how are we going to play this?" Owen asked.

"You're on defense. Stick close to our goal, since you're our slowest player. Art will run the ball, and Pam and I will play guard."

"That means Art will have to win first scrum. Can he manage that? '

Jessie nodded. "They're putting Mindy up as runner. She's fast but petite. Art can take her, as long as he's willing to overpower her."

"I'm all for equal rights," Art huffed.

Owen planted himself beside the decorated garbage can serving as goal while his teammates moved up to the halfway point. Art stood across from the wiry redhead perched beside the elastic band ball resting on a masking tape line on the floor.

"Is that a camera?" Pam asked Jessie, waiting for the whistle.

"It sure is. Top-tier's not the only one offering media exposure; mid-tier is televised too. The budget money at this level's still crap, but there's local interest and the smaller sponsors want some guarantee of exposure. That's where the budget money comes from, after all. Haven't you ever watched?"

Pam shrugged. "Too busy training."

"Put watching old episodes on your to-do list. They archive them on the public service Intranet. Do you want a metre stick or the staplers?"

"Give me the staplers. The last time I practiced with a metre stick, I broke it. Office Resources gave me a haranguing."

Jessie had just handed over the linked staplers when the whistle blew. Mindy leapt for the ball before Art could react, but he was on her before she could get away with it. He launched himself, piling into her and knocking her to the floor. A quick elbow to the face, and she was stunned enough to yield the ball. He pulled it from her semi-limp fingers.

"We're going to run close guard," Jessie told Pam as they circled in front of Art. "Art's got no defense. We need to keep him shielded"

"Whatever you say."

Pam and Jessie ran shoulder to shoulder with their older teammate, watching for Mindy's enforcers. All three of Mindy's teammates threw themselves in front of Pam, Jessie, and Art, presenting themselves as a human wall.

"We have to run ahead," Jessie called to Pam. "Make a hole! Art can dodge his way through while we keep them occupied."

"You got it!"

Pam thundered her way forward, bashing the man to her left with the staplers, his hole-punch club bouncing ineffectively off her bicep. She shouldered her way like a rhino through the one on the right, his clipboard shield negligible. Jessie used a little more finesse, clotheslining her opponent with the metrestick before he could strike with his. Both women fell into a loose pile with their targets.

"Run for it!" Pam barked.

Without hesitation, Art hurtled the pile and continued his sprint towards the goal.

"Watch it -- that one's getting up!" Jessie warned.

While the one she had tackled seemed pinned, the man Pam had clocked with the staplers had started to rise. With a grunt, Pam lurched for him, grabbing onto his shirt. It gave Art the time he needed to reach the goal and score a win.

Owen rejoined them as they celebrated.

"I was worried for a bit there, but Pam: you pulled through."

She grinned, patting Jessie on the shoulder.

"That was a great run, but we still have last round. We'll be facing a top-tier team. That'll be the real test," Art added.

"I wonder which one," Jessie said.

That thought made them all a little nervous. The day had already been rife with surprises.

"They get play pick? Shouldn't it be our turn?" Pam said.

"We defaulted into round two which gave the other team the pick. We beat a mid-tier to get into this round. Our opponents beat a lower ranking top-tier, giving them higher ranking going into round three, so they get play pick. There were more top-tiers that made it into round two than mid-tiers, so they pitted top rank at that level vs bottom rank," Jessie explained.

Art came back from reviewing the challenge board, his face red. "I thought you said Annika had been pulled because of a pregnancy."

"She was... is she here?" Jessie asked.

"She's here and we're playing against her. They have us up against Education. They'd never let her play pregnant."

"What's the call?" Pam asked, hoping the answer might shake some of the glum from her teammates' faces.

It only made things worse.

"Fire Drill."

Pam stared at their morose expressions, hoping for an explanation.

"Why the adrenaline-rush grandstand? That one's dangerous. We're not talking elbow to the nose or eye-gouging. I don't want to risk third degree burns," Owen complained.

"Maybe they're hoping we'll forfeit," Art suggested. "Most people do with that play pick."

"No." Jessie shook her head. "They've picked it to amp up sponsorship dollars. The crowd likes Fire Drill's spectacle.".

"Do you think those outfits are flame retardant?" Owen asked.

"Wait a minute," Pam said, her face now as flushed as Art's. "Are you saying we can get burned?"

"If we rush the exit, yeah. That's Annika's preferred tactic. It's why she shaves her head before the games. She's earned a few scars, but she has high pain tolerance. She doesn't panic and she has stop, drop, and roll down pat. She's made sure all of her teammates are on board. They'll all be rushing it."

"What about occupational health and safety standards? Doesn't that give us some protection?"

"Those are for plebs, Pam. Didn't you read that waiver?" Owen asked.

The look on her face said plenty. "I thought it was a media consent. Who reads the fine print before they tick, 'I agree'?"

Art rolled his eyes.

"But you said 'rush the exit' like we have another option. Do we?" Pam said.

"Fire Drill is a timed obstacle course, with a fire blocking the exit," Jessie told her. "You can grab a fire extinguisher along the way, but it'll slow you down, plus using it will cost you time. Annika always makes a straight run.

If you get there quickly, the fire's not that bad. You might get hot foot, but not much else."

"But if you're slower like Owen..?"

"The time count's based on last team member through. They already have a speed advantage. We can't afford to handicap ourselves further. Then again, one of them might not make it through if they push it."

Pam's jaw dropped. "That happens?"

"Only once," Art replied. "Third year. One guy tripped and actually landed dead centre in the fire. By the time he rolled out and they doused the flames, he had third degree burns. Apparently, you don't want to be dressed in polyester when traipsing through a blaze."

"I heard his security pass melted to his chest," Owen said.

A whistle blew.

As her team scrambled to line-up, Pam realized she'd been left with the tail-end of the relay. The lights dimmed, spotlights flashed about the office space, making their pathway seem more treacherous. Once the space before the fire escape was set ablaze, Pam bit her lip so hard she drew blood.

Gauging what she could in the shadows, she counted three obstacles constructed from assembled office equipment. She also noticed a glint, the metal top from the fire extinguisher, positioned awkwardly off to one side. With her reach she could probably grab it in passing, but she wasn't sure she could clear the obstacles with it in hand. That gave her an idea.

The fire alarm sounded: their signal to begin. Jessie sprinted for the exit, Art not far behind. Pam could tell from his tentative movements that he might balk when he reached the flames. She grabbed the fire extinguisher.

"Heads up, Jessie!"

Pam reeled back and flung the extinguisher forward with all her might. It cleared the still growing blaze and her Amazon-like teammate snatched it out of the air. Jessie activated it right away, reducing the size of the fire enough by the time Art reached it that he leapt through without hesitation. By the time Owen and Pam raced past, there was nothing left but smouldering embers.

Unfortunately, that wasn't enough.

A breathless Jessie shook her head as she reported the results. "They pushed it all the way, their slowest team member still faster than Owen. Their last guy through suffered some nasty burns, but they beat us on time."

Pam was crestfallen. "So that's it? We lose?"

Jessie grinned, wiping a stray strand of hair from her eyes. "Second place isn't exactly a loss. The budget will be tight, but we'll manage. This run may get us extra sponsors next year. We gave them a good show of teamwork. We'll make sure to spend time working on everyone's cardio next year."

"If you stick with us," Owen told Pam. "I suspect you'll be getting other offers. That was a great play."

The rest of her team agreed.

They caught sight of Education celebrating their victory. Art grimaced. "I guess this will be a year of teacher raises, school capital projects, and replenishing of supplies. Advise parents to make good use of their school nurses. At least they'll be well-funded."

Pam snorted a laugh as the door closed behind them.

Paul Carberry

Paul Carberry is a huge proponent of the horror genre and its place in literature. He has two children, daughter Dana and son Rick, with his wife Leah.

Paul has published three novels with Engen Books: *Zombies on the Rock: Outbreak*, *Zombies on the Rock: The Viking Trail*, and *Zombies on the Rock: The Republic of Newfoundland*. He has also had numerous short stories featured in publication, including 'The Light of Cabot Tower,' 'Into the Forest,' and 'Halloween Mummers.'

His fourth novel, focusing on shark attacks, will be released in 2020.

He brings with him a reprint of his chiller classic, 'Halloween Mummers,' as well as a new fantasy story, 'The Charybdis and Scylla.'

Halloween Mummers

Jessie snuggled her head into Alex's chest, covering her legs with a blanket. Alex sat in the corner of couch and Jessie made herself comfortable on the rest of the couch. They were watching a movie on a TV that hung above the fireplace. The curling flames swayed and flickered, casting long shadows across the hardwood floor. The wood fire sent its warmth and light throughout the living room while two mugs of coffee sat on the coffee table in front of the mantle. Outside the wind howled, making the seams of the house creek as the rain pattered off the windows. A dull orange glow from the hanging pumpkin lights in the window caught Jessie's platinum blonde hair. Alex stared at the television intently, paying close attention to the horror movie he was watching. Jessie didn't like scary movies, but the slow stream of trick or treaters had stopped hours ago.

"What an awful night for trick or treating." Jessie tried to start a conversation so she wouldn't have to listen to the dreadful noises on the TV. After a few awkward moment of silence, Jessie looked at Alex's scruffy face. His black rimmed glasses rested on his crooked nose which had been broken in a fight outside of the bar last night. The skin around one of his eyes had turned black and was nearly swollen shut, but he managed to keep track of everything that was happening in his movie.

"I said it's an awful night." Jessie's voice had shown her frustration more then she had meant it to.

Alex turned his head to look at the bowl of treats next to the door. "Depends."

"Depends on what, Alex?"

"Depends on how you look at things, I guess." Alex turned his head back to continue watching his movie.

Jessie knew he was headed somewhere with that vague statement. If she wasn't so bored, she would have left it alone, but having nothing better to do, she decided to play along. "Well, it's wet and cold out. I mean, that to me seems like a terrible night to be outside going door to door looking for candy."

"Exactly."

"Exactly? Are you agreeing with me or did you have a point to make?" Jessie made no effort to hide her frustration now.

"Well, look at the bowl and tell me what you see?" A smirk on his face made a wave of wrinkles under his eyes.

"A bowl full of candies and chocolate bars." Jessie wondered where he was going with this.

"Exactly."

"Exactly what?" Jessie groaned.

"Think about it. If every kids' parents bought treats to hand out like we did, then the kid got to stay home tonight, watch a scary movie, and eat those treats without having to put in any of the work." Alex stretched out for his coffee, but couldn't reach it with Jessie resting on him. Jessie propped herself up enough to get Alex his coffee. "Since you're already up, you mind grabbing me some of those candy bars?" Alex laughed.

Jessie gave Alex a playful punch in the stomach. "You jerk." Jessie pushed the blanket aside and put her feet on the hardwood floor. The fire hadn't been burning long enough yet to warm the floorboards and a chill ran up her backside. She made her way over to the bowl and looked down at all the treats. "What do you want?"

"Just bring it all over, I'm sure we aren't getting anyone else," Alex called out from the couch.

Jessie looked over to find he had pulled the blanket over himself. She grabbed the bowl and just as she turned to walk back, a loud knock on the door startled her. "Looks like you will have to share," Jessie teased.

Jessie opened the door and was startled by a gust of wind that pushed the door all the way open. Three people stood on the porch dressed up like mummers from Christmas time. The first one was a rather tall man wearing a flowered dress with a pair of polka dotted men's boxers pulled on over the dress. His hairy legs ran into a pair of yellow rubber boots. A white sheet with triangle eyeholes and a frown drawn with red lipstick covered the face and was tucked into his dress. The second person was much shorter and wore a black and blue plaid jacket over jean coveralls with the pant legs tucked into green rubber boots. They wore a pillowcase with ragged eyeholes and a frown drawn in black marker to cover their face. The last mummer stood in the back wearing a lacy red nightgown over a black sweater with a white hood covering their face as well. Large black circles were painted around the eyeholes and an innocent smile was painted in red where the face should have been. "Any mummers 'loud in?" one of them said.

Jessie laughed. "Wrong holiday, guys, but I love the

costumes." None of the mummers had bags for trick or treating. "Maybe you should take those bags off your head so you can collect some candy." Jessie held out the candy dish.

"No one will let us in?" one of the mummers piped up. "You'll regret that."

"What did you say?" Jessie couldn't believe what she heard. "Alex, come over here."

"Let's see if the neighbours are any nicer." The mummers turned to leave just as Alex got to the door.

"What's wrong, dear?" Alex said. "What are they wearing?" he said as he noticed their strange attire.

"One of them said, you'll regret that." Jessie could feel her hand trembling.

"Regret what?" Alex reached out and took the bowl of candy from Jessie's hand.

"Don't be a jerk, Alex; what if they had tried to force their way inside?" Jessie was glad they were gone, but she still felt crept out by the whole encounter.

Alex didn't say anything; he just shrugged his shoulders.

"Thanks, dear, I feel so much safer." Jessie pushed her way past Alex and headed back to the couch. Alex unplugged the pumpkin lights in the window and drew the curtains closed before sitting back down next to Jessie. "I can't watch this, I'm changing the channel."

Alex started to object, but must have seen the frightened look in Jessie's eye and just nodded in agreement. Jessie knew she wasn't going to be able to get to sleep anytime soon without one of her sleeping pills. "Could you please get me one of my bedtime pills?"

"Sure." Alex headed upstairs while Jessie surfed the channels for anything that wasn't related to Halloween.

Everything had a Halloween theme tonight, so she settled for one of the comedy shows airing their kooky holiday special. Alex returned with a pill and he sat back down on the couch. Jessie tilted her head back and threw the pill down her throat; she couldn't wait to fall asleep and get this night over with. She put her head back on Alex's chest and after a few minutes drifted off into a restless sleep.

A loud knock on the door startled Jessie out of her sleep and she nearly jumped to her feet. "What was that?"

"It's probably the neighbours coming to apologize for the loud screaming." Alex pushed his way off the couch and headed towards the door. Jessie's head was muddled and she felt groggy from her pill. The door creaked open. "Can I help you?"

"I'm looking for my friend, have you seen him?" An eerie voice came from outside.

"It's a little late to be trick or treating, even for someone your age," Alex barked back.

"Who is it, Alex?"

"I'm sorry, we didn't let your friends in earlier and I'm not letting you in either." Alex closed the door and locked it.

"Who is it?" Jessie could feel her nerves fraying, sending erratic impulses throughout her body. She wanted to run to the phone, but she couldn't move or control her body from shaking.

"One of those people dressed up like a mummer." Alex's voice was filled with anger. Rage was surfacing in him once again, the same temper that had gotten him the black eye at the bar. Alex stormed over to the window and opened the curtains. "What the hell is she doing?" Alex raced over to the door and put his shoes on.

"Alex, don't leave me here alone," Jessie pleaded, feeling the dread grow deep inside.

Alex didn't listen to her pleas, throwing the door open. "Call the cops." Alex slammed the door shut behind him.

Jessie jumped up and ran over to lock the door. She walked into the kitchen to get the phone, but it wasn't on the charger. Jessie cursed Alex; he probably left it lying around somewhere. She scoured the kitchen table and counter tops for the phone, but it was nowhere in sight. Jessie headed back into the living room to get her cell phone.

"Where did I leave it?" Jessie couldn't think straight, the effects of the drugs still clouding her thoughts. She looked over the coffee table and the bookcase to no avail; her phone wasn't in plain view. Jessie could hear Alex cursing at someone outside.

Fear gripped her heart and made her want to hide under the blanket, but she needed to see what Alex was screaming at. She put her hand on curtains and started to pull them back slowly, terror hindering her motor skills. Outside was nearly pitch black except for the dull yellow glow of the streetlights. The doorknob jingled as someone tried to turn it, then a loud knock threatened to break the door down.

"Alex." Jessie ran over to the door to let Alex in. She threw the door open and nearly toppled over backwards.

"Have you seen my friend yet?" The mummer with the smile stood on the porch.

"Get out of here!" Jessie screamed franticly, unable to summon the courage to move. Only a few feet separated the two.

"Are you sure you haven't seen him? He said he

would meet me here." The mysterious voice made Jessie's skin crawl. The mummer started to move towards Jessie methodically, her hands by her side. Jessie noticed dark red specks over the mummer's neck and nightgown. The mummer inched closer now, slowing raising her hands towards Jessie. The intruder was close enough now that Jessie could see her green eyes staring back at her.

"Get out of here." Alex grabbed the prowler by the shoulders and hurtled her off the porch and onto the wet lawn. He slammed the door shut behind. "Have you called the cops?"

"I can't find the phone." Jessie was nearly in tears. Alex raced into the kitchen and she could hear him rummaging through magazines on the kitchen table and cursing under his breath. "What's going on?" Alex rushed back into the living room and headed straight for the couch with a panicked look on his face. He started ripping the cushions off the couch and looking underneath it as well. "Alex?"

"My cell phone's dead, where's yours?" Alex flipped over the last cushion.

"I don't know?" Jessie shuddered, her heart palpitating.

Alex darted upstairs to look the phone. In the silence, Jessie could hear something tapping against the window. She just turned away from the window, praying that the sound would go away. She stared into the fire and her heart jumped into her throat; she could see her phone melting on top of the burning ashes in the fireplace.

A pair of hands grabbed Jessie from behind and spun her around.

"Why is the bedroom window left open?" Alex shook Jessie back and forth, trying to bring her back to her senses, but all that escaped her lips were silent gasps. Alex turned to look towards the deliberate tapping at the window. He headed straight for the curtains; Jessie reached out to try and stop him, but her legs wouldn't budge. Alex tossed open the curtains revealing the mummer with the smile standing there, tapping a pair of keys against the glass.

"Get out of here!" Alex yelled furiously.

The mummer stopped tapping the glass and pointed her finger at Jessie. Alex craned his neck and followed the aim of her finger. "Jessie!"

Jessie spun around and jumped back as the mummer with the red lipstick frown stood in the kitchen. Alex pushed his way past her and met the assailant head on. Alex didn't see the kitchen knife in his hand, but Jessie could see the end of the blade sticking out through Alex's back. A stream of blood slowly flowed down his stomach and started to pool on the floor.

Alex turned his head towards Jessie. "Run." Blood gurgled in his throat as he fell to the ground.

Jessie's instincts finally took over and she rushed towards the front door, but the knob was turning. She could hear the lock opening so she changed directions and dashed up the stairs. She looked behind her as the front door opened and just as she reached the top, she felt a strong blow to the side of the face, sending her tumbling down the stairs. The world spun around as she toppled head over heels, a barrage of pain shooting from every nerve ending as she descended the stairwell. Jessie crashed into the feet of the smiling mummer, who reached down and pinned her to the floor. Jessie thrashed around, trying to break her assailant's grasp, but she couldn't. Her ankle had been broken during her fall, the bone jutting through the skin. The stairs creaked as the other intruder made his way down, dragging a sledgehammer behind him. The heavy metal head banged loudly off each step.

"Why are you doing this?" Jessie pleaded to the three mummers. The mummer with the black frown pulled off his hood; she had no idea who he was or what he wanted. He just smiled at her for a moment. "Please let me go?" The hoodless mummer raised the sledgehammer above his head and held it there, staring down at her. "What do you want?"

"You should have just let us in."

The Charybdis and Scylla

Wave after wave rocked the Athenian galley, salt water washing over the deck, soaking the men below. Their tired groans only broken off by the alarmed cries as the ship tilted too far to one side, then the next. Buried behind a jet black sky crowded with threatening rain clouds, the moon afforded the Captain little light. If he didn't discover a haven soon, they would all drown in the briny deep. Ahead, nestled in between two towering cliffs, a black chasm opened up.

A narrow strait offered shelter from the raging storm, the cliff walls breaking the waves. The shallow waters were as black as the midnight sky, the moonlight dying at the surface. Rain pummeled the Captain's face, the gale whipping it sideways. He felt the ship listing far to the port side. Tidal waves continued to splash over the deck. The ocean was eager to sink his ship. Rumors of the terrible creatures that lived within those caves remained secluded in the dreadful darkness within the narrow strait. Odysseus had confronted Charybdis and Scylla and survived to recount the tale. Determined to make a name for himself, the Captain could think of no better way. With no alternative option, he swung the keel and steered the Athenian galley into the narrow strip of paradise, praying it wasn't a mirage. Swept near the craggy shore, oars banged against the jutting rocks as they invaded the shallow depths.

Beneath the glossy black surface, something slithered underneath the boat. Oars ripped from the men's hands without warning, leaving them scrambling below deck. A gaping hole opened up in the blackness, water churning in a frenzy around its edges. Desperately, the Captain struggled to maneuver his ship away from the growing whirl pool, howling at his brothers to paddle harder, the ship spun out of control. If they sailed to the other side, they would be clear of the torrential pull. Water sprayed over the deck, splashing into his face. Screams erupted down below as the wood splintered. Loud, gushing water streamed through the galley, sucking men through the opening, the current dragging them away. Terrified men scrambled to get on deck, their eyes filled with dread, their cries choked with salt water.

From his perch, the Captain watched his men jump overboard, abandoning ship. Their limbs cut the water, swimming with a purpose towards the distant shore. Caught in the moonlight, a reptilian monster rose from the shallow water. Four long necks, each with a horrendous set of snapping jaws, slithered in the air like a serpent. Scales, dripping with water, glistened a rich emerald green, covered the Scylla's torso. Behind him now, the Charybdis opened its jaws wide and guzzled the shallow water. The galley brought up along the bottom, spilling on to its side and tossing the Captain into the hollow sea. A torrent of rushing water sucked him towards the gaping mouth. He tried to scream; the sound deadened by a throat full of water. His fingers scraped along the rugged bottom, probing for something to clutch on to. Pieces of splintered wood from the galley, swept up by the current, jabbed at the men captured in the swell. Trails of blood ran in the water, pouring into the Charybdis's open mouth, driving it mad with hunger.

Agonized shrieks rose from the water. Bodies, snatched from the water, gasping for air as the Scylla plunged its heads into the churning water. Men wiggled beneath the many jaws of the fearsome beast, thrashing their arms and screaming out in misery. Sharp, jagged teeth in its jaws sliced through flesh and bone with familiarity. Limbs fell from the sky, splashing sea water and blood high into the sky. The Scylla's entire mass hide within a murky cavern, the full mass of the demon still slithering from its hiding space. It climbed the rugged cliff side; the rocks trembled beneath its mass. Crumbled pieces tumbled into the water, landing on top of the men working to swim to shore. Bodies floated face-down in the shallow water. Mangled bodies, battling desperately to hang onto life, failed hopelessly. The Scylla feasted upon the sailors like a gruesome buffet.

Sickened by the crunching bones the Captain vomited, his mouth full of salt water and bile. Urgently, he reached out and grasped an oar that had been drifting past him. Sucked into the spinning whirlpool of water, an excruciating sensation gripped him. The back of his legs and heels getting cut up by the rocks. A gaping black void, rimmed by viscous white fangs, waited for him. Other members of his crew thrashed against the current ahead of him. He listened in horror at their anguished moans. As they entered the Charybdis mouth, they tried to cling to the edge, razor-sharp teeth piercing into their flesh. The Captain glowered at the immense oval black eye beneath the churning water staring back at him. Instinctively, the

Captain jabbed the oar into the creature's eye. A hideous roar erupted from the beast's throat as the wooden tip punctured the creature's eye. Water sprouted from the monsters mouth, it regurgitated the last few men with a disgusting belch. A wave of blood swept over the Captain, knocking him backwards. Chewed morsels of flesh fouled the water, a piece rushed down the Captain's mouth as he inhaled in a mouthful of water. The stench of death hung like a fog in the air. The Charybdis dove back into its cave to tend to its wound.

A laughing fit gripped the Captain. The water level rose once more, forcing him to tread water. Ripples in the water carried the remnants of his crew to the surface, making the water thick and viscous. He heard the Scylla grinding bones beneath its teeth behind him. Not wishing to be devoured by the creature, he dove beneath the water. He opened his mouth wide, filling his lungs with the salty sea water.

Peter J Foote

Peter J. Foote is a bestselling speculative fiction writer from Nova Scotia, Canada. He runs the FictionFirst Used Books, specializing in fantasy & sci-fi titles. He also cosplays with his wife, and alternates between red wine and coffee as the mood demands.

Many of Peter's stories are a reflection of his personal life, as he is a firm believer in the adage that a writer should write what they know.

Peter's work has twice been awarded the Kit Sora Flash Fiction Prize: once in March 2018 and again in September 2018. Peter holds the distinction of being one of only three authors to be featured in all the modern From the Rock collections to date.

In total, Peter has been featured in over two dozen publications, with interest in his short fiction worldwide.

As the founder of the group "Genre Writers of Atlantic Canada," Peter believes that the writing community is stronger when it works together.

He brings with him two new stories, the science-fiction flash fiction 'Reflections' and the fantasy tale, 'The Promise.'

Reflections

"I'm scared Ramsey, what if it's... gone?"

Ramsey pats her brother's shoulder, fallout dust rises. "It'll be fine, you've been careful and changed your filters as Pa taught us."

"But what if I have a leak like Pa and don't know it?"

"Pa always made sure we had the best filters and used castoffs for himself. It's been three months since we've had a chance for fresh air and we'll not waste it. Now take off your mask."

Shaky hands unclasp the gas mask, peeling it away from filthy skin. Looking into the cracked mirror, Drew cries at his reflection.

The Promise

"This one Papa, it looks like Mama," says eight-year-old Lottie, perched on her dad's shoulders.

Ernest grips his daughter's skinny legs so tight that the coal dust, impregnated into the palms of his hands, leaves faint black smudges on her bare legs. Smiling up at his daughter, Ernest thinks to himself: *It's the first joy she's shown in the real world since Fern passed, I dreaded I was losing her, too.*

"How much for the doll Master Merchant? It resembles my wife."

If the merchant thinks it odd that a coal miner in a threadbare and patched miners bib with his daughter on his shoulders is standing in his stall particular, he shows no sign once the matter of money becomes involved.

"That there relic survived the flooding without a scrape, her eyes are as green and vivid as they were when first created, her straw-colored hair still has a beautiful luster, and I'll not accept fewer than fourteen silver pennies for it."

Fourteen silver pennies! That's two month's wages in the mine! Ernest thinks to himself. His dismay must have reflected on his face as the merchant sneers and with a nimble motion plucks the doll from Lottie's grasp.

"Papa!" Lottie cries as her tiny arms ache to reach after the doll that reminds the little girl of the parent she lost last winter.

"Please Master Merchant, can we not come to an arraignment?" Ernest pleads, his expression a reflection to that of his daughter.

The merchant opens his mouth, recognizes the sell-sword standing beside the miner and the fire in his eyes dims as he coughs into his fist and replies; "What arraignment? I don't need a hole dug!" The merchant laughs at his own joke.

"What if I told you I had specialized skills that might be of value to you?"

"Ernest, don't do this..." Harold the sell-sword hisses in a sharp tone.

Waving off the concerns from his brother-in-law, Ernest casts glances over both shoulders before leaning in and saying; "I read and write, as a prosperous merchant that must be of value, you won't have to use the church for those tasks."

The merchants' reaction is instantaneous. Backing into his apprentice who bumps against displays of pre-rising treasures, the ensuing crash isn't enough to take the merchant's eyes off the trio in front of him. Thrusting back his sealskin cape, the merchant grabs hold of the huge brass anchor hanging around his neck and, in a resounding voice, exclaims; "I'm true to the faith, the Lord of the Waves is my savior. It is his judgment that learning is alone pure in the hands of his Watchers who oversee and preserve us."

As the crowd sees the disturbance, Harold grabs Ernest and tugs him aside, causing Lottie to wobble on her father's shoulders.

Hissing in his ear, Harold says "You damn idiot, why did you do that? Now we'll be lucky to get out with our skin."

Lottie grabs her father's shoulders until her fingers are white. "Papa! Why is that man yelling and is Uncle Harold frightened? I want to leave this place, please Papa!"

Harold drags Ernest out of the market, through the sea of pointing fingers and whispering shoppers, they fail to notice the merchant grab his assistant, speak into his ear, and dispatch him running with a boot to his backside.

"It's people like that which created the world the way it is, as long as he's fed and protected he doesn't give a damn about..." Ernest breaks off as Lottie cries "Papa, I'm scared!" and Ernest stops his rush that threatens to dislodge his daughter from his shoulders and lowers her into a hug as Harold scans the lane behind them searching for pursuit.

Holding his pale and frightened daughter in a strong embrace, the anger leaves Ernest's face as he strokes her hair, saying: "I'm sorry, darling. I didn't mean to lose my temper. I wanted our day at the market to be special, I only get to visit you once a month." Lottie stops her shaking and allows her father's embrace to enfold her.

With Harold standing between the huddled pair and the street going back to the market, he scans the smoke-filled skies alight with the glow of the setting sun. "I think we should get Lottie back to the boarding house, the sun is going down and we don't want to risk being spotted on the street after curfew."

Raising his tear-stained face from his daughter's shoulder, Ernest watches his brother-in-law standing guard over them his scarred hand slowing pulling out the steel blade at his hip and thrusting it home. *I know Harold is as frustrated, Fern was his sister, but his life as a sell-sword can't make a home for Lottie any better than mine in the coal pit. I know the boarding house is little better than a child prison, but it's better than Lottie being adopted and brainwashed by the church into a pawn so they can maintain control.*

When Harold looks back at them, Ernest catches his eye and gives his brother-in-law a somber nod, and says to his daughter: "Your Uncle Harold is right, let's bring you back, I have to find the convoy back to the mine if I wish to save my job."

With each of the men holding one of Lottie's hands, the group makes their way through the emptying streets of Tidney Town; at their backs, the shadows lengthen.

Though streets of crumbling asphalt laid more than a generation before they were born, between homes and shops of rough timber built upon ancient concrete foundations the group walks, the adults doing their best to distract the young girl from the filth and decay as they enter the sprawling slums of the town.

Amid recounting a tale about a rancher and his runaway pig who spooked a merchants pony causing a rampage at the town gate last week, Harold spies a shadow detach itself from an alleyway and a figure strides into the roadway and halts in front of the group.

Stepping in front of the father and daughter, Harold pulls back his grey wool cloak and places his hand to the blade at his belt. "If you know what's healthy for you, you'd heave off this instant!" Harold says, his powerful voice sharp enough to cut stone.

A throaty female laugh answers Harold as a young woman in a sealskin cloak, polished boots, and well-made gloves walks forward and pauses, the golden medallion of an anchor around her neck, topped with a radiant eye that captures the evening light.

As if scorched, Harold moves his hand away from his blade and bows, his face pale. "Lady Watcher, I didn't realize. We don't see many of the church in this area of the town, please forgive me."

Her eyes slide off of Harold as she saunters up to Ernest not halting until their noses almost touch. She says: "You can read and write?"

Ernest gives a slight nod, mindful not to touch the Watcher, the penalty of death for touching a member of the church being exercised in the town.

Her eyes twinkle as she steps back and thrusts a gloved hand into the pocket of her robe. Pulling out the blue leather ritual book with the gold anchor of the church on the cover, she opens it to a random page and thrusts it in front of Ernest's face "Read".

Ernest risks a brief glance at Harold who shrugs his shoulders, Ernest squeezes his daughter's shoulder and recites aloud; "Waves are the voice of the Lord, they send us the food of his body, they carry our ships upon his back. They are his pulse, his loving heartbeat."

The Watcher snaps the book closed, causing the group to jump, and as she replaces her ritual she asks; "How is it you can read, you're not churched trained?"

Ernest shakes his head. "It's a family tradition, parents teach their children to read and write, my great-grandmother was a teacher before the waters rose and civilization fled."

She holds up a gloved hand to cut off Ernest "Before

the Lord of the Waves washed aside the evil and corrupt leaving behind only the pure," she says.

"I stand corrected Lady Watcher," Ernest replies, though he meets her eye as he speaks.

The Watcher laughs; "Oh I like you, you have a spine, though it must get bent spending a life underground grubbing for coal, only allowed in the town one weekend a month, what kind of future will that provide for your girl?"

Ernest drops his eyes towards the broken pavement at his feet, his face crimson in shame, still, he holds his daughter tight against his body.

The Watcher goes on, "They squander your skills in the mines, I hear black lung is a slow and arduous death."

His face turning blood red, Ernest keeps his voice calm. "I have no ambition to enter the church, I fear I would make an unsatisfactory Acolyte."

"No? Well, there are other ways to serve the Lord of the Waves. I demand your skills for a particular project." Holding up her gloved hand to forestall the objection on Ernest's lips, she goes on. "You are being given a once in a lifetime chance here, a chance at a future for yourself," her eyes stray down to Lottie, "And your girl. Meet me at the west gate at low twelve and tell no one, you won't receive another chance like this, I promise."

With that, she turns away from Ernest but pierces Harold with her eyes causing him to rock back on his heels. "Just because YOU don't see members in this neighborhood, doesn't mean we aren't here." As she strides back into the dark of the alleyway, several other shadows detach from around the group and accompany her.

"I'm not sure this is a good idea, Ernest," Harold whispers to Ernest as the pair make their way through the darkened lanes, the moonlight casting narrow shadows behind them, but Ernest isn't listening.

Reflecting about the somber parting he'd had with Lottie at the boarding house and the wretched conditions his frail daughter was living in, *I'm not the only one failing by inches. What kind of life did she have ahead of her? Scrubbing other folk's clothes for a lifetime? Taken as a rich man's mistress when older, or even sooner by some. Or brainwashed and used by the church to control the thoughts and fate of everybody within these walls.* "We need to escape this town..." Ernest murmurs to himself.

The church bell strikes low twelve as Ernest and Harold come to the courtyard in front of the gate. The massive gate formed of peeled logs sits between the thick steel walls that envelop the town. Ernest has heard the tales that these giant steel blocks were shipping containers that perched atop ships by the hundreds as they crisscrossed the waters of the world, but the scale of such a feat is mind-boggling. The Church states these are a gift from the Lord of the Waves and any conjecture of the world before the Rising is heretical, and punishable by drowning.

Shaking off the myths and fantasies of the former world, Ernest concentrates on the here and now. There are two groups at the locked gate, half a dozen militia members, and the Watcher flanked by two huge church guards. Dressed in hardened leather armor and bearing wave-bladed swords at their sides, riot guns in their hands, and traveling packs upon their backs, the anchor brand on their cheeks highlighted by the flickering torchlight. While out-numbered two to one, the Lady Watcher's group has the advantage as the militia members huddle behind their officer. Ernest and Harold are close enough to overhear his shaking voice.

"Lady Watcher, I am sorry but the laws imposed down by the church are clear; I lock the gates at sundown, and only church lead convoys can enter the wilds. It is alone by the shielding grace of the Lord of the Waves that evil stays outside." The Officer performs the sign of the anchor upon his breast a shaking hand.

Patting the thick arm of her guard as if he would a hound, the Watcher saunters towards the trembling officer tugging off her leather gloves as she goes. As she beams down into the pale face of the officer, she says; "There is my convey coming now" as she brandishes one of her bare hands towards Harold and Ernest, "and here is my dispensation from Bishop Campbell" as she thrusts a folded parchment she's drawn from inside her cloak into the shaking hands of the officer. Even from this distance, Ernest can identify the thick crimson wax seal of the Anchor of the Church stamped upon it.

With clumsy motions, the officer unfolds the parchment and does his best to study it in the flickering torchlight. Ernest watches the officer's bewildered face as struggles to make out the contents written on it. Snatching the parchment out of his hands, folding it up and shoving it back into the folds of her clothing, gone is her pleasant manner as she snaps; "Open the gate now and let me through or you will discover yourself at the Widow's Stones at low tide for judgment from the Lord of the Waves." The threat of a slow death in the eyes of the townsfolk motivates the militia officer as he and his squad crank open the gate, allowing the group of five to slip out of Tidney Town.

A couple hundred paces down the gravel roadway, the Watcher holds up her hand to halt the group as she rounds on Harold. "I don't recall requesting you on this mission, what's stopping me from sending you back?" With his hands still at his sides, well aware of the two guards at her back and the riot guns in their hands, Harold replies, "Ernest's family, I promised my sister I would watch after him and my niece as best I could, and I keep my promises. Also, Lady Watcher, it seems you don't wish to attract unnecessary attention since you're leaving when few eyes are watching and without a large entourage as befits your station." His message conveyed, Harold bows his head in deference.

The sweet laugh out of the lips that just moments ago menaced a man's life startles both Ernest and Harold. "You are a remarkable family your little group, here Miner, what do you make of this?" The Lady Watcher once again removes the parchment from the folds of her sealskin cloak and tosses it to Ernest. With enough moonlight to seize the folded parchment out of the air, Ernest unfolds it and inspects the writing.

"But, but this is a sanction for the merchants' guild to peddle their wares at next month's lunar festival..." Ernest mutters.

"That's correct, but that idiot didn't realize, I doubt he could read or write more than his name. Knowledge is power, and I'm determined to grab as much as I can hold." She says as she turns away and strides off into the night.

The stink of Tidney Town behind him, Ernest hastens after the Watcher and the rest of the group. Filling his lungs with the crisp salt air of the ocean, and relishing in the powerful waves against the nearby shore, he can almost forget the danger that his foolish outburst has placed his loved ones in, almost.

"Several weeks ago," the Lady Watcher begins as the odd group marches through the night. "When my patrol was defending our borders from those untouched by the grace of the Lord of the Waves, we stumbled upon a cleft in a hillside the result of a recent earthquake." Ernest knows of the quake, they lost 46 men and women in the coal mines that day in cave-ins. Shaking off the memory of hauling out dead bodies that hours before were companions, and grateful that it wasn't him leaving Lottie all alone, Ernest almost misses what the Lady Watcher says next.

"We investigated the opening and discovered that an ancient building stood there, long since collapsed and overgrown. Within were the remnants of many ancient books, more than I've seen outside the Holy Temple." Without meaning too, Ernest finds himself drawn to the story, and what that place might have been before the world got its revenge upon humanity.

"As I said," she continues "Knowledge is power, and I'm determined to get my that power, and you will serve me. You two will search the tunnels and bring forth whatever books you may discover. By the grace of the Lord of the Waves, I might even manage an Arch Bishop position for myself." The cold, calculating hunger in her tone makes the bitter night air feel warm and makes Ernest's blood turn to ice.

With the rising sun going up at their backs, Ernest shuffles his feet at the back of the group, his breathing coming in gulps as he feels the black tar that has taken up residence in his lungs rattle around. *How long do I have? I promised Fern that would give our daughter a future and I can't do that if I'm dead.* Ernest thinks to himself as he sees Harold drop back to walk alongside him.

The pair walk side by side through the wasteland of the earth, a world scoured by storms and corrupted by man, only now is nature securing a foothold and healing.

"You stay behind me Ernest, I don't trust her as far as I can spit," Harold says under his breath.

"Nor do I, but what choice do I have? Lottie is all I have left in this world, and I must do everything in my power to give her a life. If that means giving the church knowledge so be it, I'm not a hero and this isn't a story." Ernest might have added more, but a wave of coughing overwhelms him.

Placing his arm around his Ernest, Harold helps him catch up to the Lady Watcher and her guards who have halted at the base of a modest hill. The hill possesses nothing to distinguish it from the dozens of others they have passed, low with a smattering of gnarled fir trees struggling to find purchase in the rocky terrain. The Lady Watcher glares at the pair as they catch up before pointing to a jumble granite boulders.

"The entrance is between those stones, but first gather firewood and we'll set up camp. Mind you keep close, wild dogs roam these regions." With no chance to catch his breath, but knowing complaining would make matters worse, Ernest trudges off with Harold to gather the sparse pickings to start a fire.

"What is that stink? Reminds me of the sewage pits at the coal mines" Ernest says wrinkling his nose while struggling not to drop the armload of twisted branches he could locate in the harsh landscape.

"You're not too far off," Harold says as he uses one of his branches to poke into the loose soil. His stick lifts a pale and decomposing arm. "Wild dogs don't bury bodies, and neither do bandits. Unless I miss my guess, we're looking at the remains of our Lady Watchers patrol that found this cave. We need to make sure we don't end up the same."

Turning aside from the dead bodies, Ernest sighs; "I see no way out of this but to continue, if we run, they'll cut us down, and even if we get away, there's no way back into town without her. I'm not leaving Lottie, she's all I have left."

Nodding, Harold lets the limb drop back into its shallow grave, kicks soil over it before picking up his bundle of firewood and trudging back to the camp.

Walking back to the camp, Ernest can't help but note that the guards have their riot guns cradled in their arms ready for use and the Lady Watcher is watching them with an intense stare making her brow to wrinkle. "I hope you didn't stray, we ran into bandits the last time we were here and I'd hate to lose you." She says, though her tone conveys no such concern.

"No Lady Watcher, we didn't need to go far to find what we needed," Ernest responds, his eyes downcast and tone subdued.

She glares at the pair for a long moment as if struggling to detect any hidden meaning in their words, before waving her hand at a simple circle of stones and says, "Start a fire, then prepare to go into the cave."

"This is your chance to shine," The Lady Watcher says as one guard thrusts a seal-oil lamp into Harold's hands, the other one covering them with the riot gun.

"Remember, any books you can recover, but focus on ones of learning and machines. May the Lord of the Waves guide you and protect you." The Lady Watcher says as she holds up the golden anchor hanging from her neck.

Harold and Ernest look at each other, Ernest nods and with Harold holding the lamp in front of him, and the pair slip between the granite boulders and into the blackness of the ruins.

A powerful stench hits the pair as they invade the humid air of the cave, and their leather boots sink into a gooey mess. "Bats," says Ernest as he looks to the ceiling above. "They're common at some old mines, and the Church values their droppings, something to do with guns I think." Taking his eyes off the ceiling, Ernest gets his first proper look at the surrounding cavern.

It's obvious that this was once an extensive building from the time before the Rising, filled with shattered glass and steel threaded concrete common in such structures. Small bones moldy and chewed cover the parts of the uneven floor that aren't littered in bat droppings.

At the edge of the lamplight, Harold spies a large book and points to Ernest, moisture swells the pages as if the words within are seeking to escape. Ernest tries to make out the lettering on the cover to no avail, and when he tries to pick up the book, it dissolves into mush in his hands.

Rubbing his hands upon his stained mining coveralls, Ernest shakes his head. "It's useless here, the damp has ruined everything, we might have better luck deeper."

At the end of the cavern, the ceiling dips low forcing Harold to watch his head, and lamplight illuminates a square hole in the wall, rodent tracks through the dust cover the floor. The hallway branches, to the right it's a jumble of collapsed concrete and fractured glass and mirror, the lamplight reflecting off it showing a spacious chamber at the end. On the left, the archway has disintegrated leaving behind a cramped shaft that would require they crawl. Turning to the right, Harold jumps when Ernest grabs his forearm in a vice-like grip and hisses "No!" Pointing to the top of the glass-strewn corridor he explains;"That's a widow-maker tunnel, one false step and that ceiling will come down on you, the stacked glass is like a house of cards."

"I see it now, though not without you pointing, that could have been messy," Harold adds in a lighthearted tone that echoes through the ruin.

The absurdity of the situation overwhelms the pair as the slip into a fit of nervous laughter, after rubbing tears from dust-covered faces, they shift their attention to the left tunnel.

Wiping the grime off of the archway, letters of black glass reflect in the lamplight. "What does it say, Ernest?" Kneeling down to get a better look, Ernest traces the letters with his coal-blackened fingers and says; "The Sherry D. Ramsey Memorial Section." He reiterates it several times to himself before turning to his companion. "I think we're in a library." Seeing the puzzled expression upon Harold's face, he says; "A shrine of books, a storehouse of knowledge accessible to everybody and not dominated by the church."

Taking the lamp from Harold, Ernest says "Stay, I'll know what to look for." And with that, wriggles into the tunnel, leaving Harold alone.

Coughing and the sounds of scratching of fabric upon

rock issuing from the tunnel alert Harold to Ernest's return. He would never say it, but being alone in the dark is much scarier than confronting a cutthroat in the streets of Tidney Town.

Moments later, the swaying light of the lamp comes out of the tunnel resting on top of a stack of books being pushed by Ernest. Even covered in rat dropping, dust and cobwebs can't cover the grin from Ernest's face. "It's treasure trove, Harold! Hundreds of books in a maze of tumbled shelves, more than a person could study in a lifetime, in a dozen lifetimes."

"Look here," the excitement in Ernest's voice is infectious and even Harold forgets the dire situation they are in. "Siege warfare in the medieval ages, Science experiments for kids, and principles of electricity. I know these will be of value, take them to her, I need to rest a minute the air is stale in there."

Gathering up the handful of ancient tomes under his arm, Harold makes his way back to the entrance the swinging lamp guiding his path. He's not surprised to discover that the Lady Watcher and her guards have entered the cavern themselves, the world of the church doesn't work on trust. With their own lamps at their feet, Harold can't miss the gleam of the steel barrels as the riot guns track his passage towards them. Harold places the lamp at his feet and passes the bundle of books to the Watcher.

The sharp intake of her breath tells Harold that Ernest was correct and that these books are of use, maybe enough to buy their lives.

"Are there more of these?" The Watcher asks, her voice taut with emotion.

"Yes Lady Watcher, Ernest says dozens if not hundreds."

"Excellent, this is more than sufficient to warrant a full-scale expedition." Turning to her guards she says, "See to the other one, we have no..." a deep rumble drowns out whatever else she said, it shakes the whole cavern, panicking the roosting bats as they streak past the group and fly outside.

"Ernest!" Seizing his lamp and dashing back the way he came, heedless of the rain of stones falling all around him, Harold fails to notice the Watcher sending her two guards after him their riot guns at the ready.

Blinded by the clouds of dust and shifting shadows thrown by the lamp, Harold scrambles over some fallen rocks and makes it to the archway where he left Ernest minutes ago.

Now split and caved in, the archway lies atop of Ernest pinning him at the abdomen. Kneeling beside Ernest, Harold reaches out a shaking hand to take a pulse, only to have Ernest cough out a mouth of blood and peer up at his companion and smile.

"Load shifted, I might have bumped something, can't feel my legs," Ernest says, his breathing ragged and labored.

"Just don't move," noticing the guards have come up behind him, Harold continues "See help is here, we'll have back to town before sundown."

"You were always an awful liar," Ernest says, his mouth caked with blood. Reaching an arm under himself, Ernest struggles to pull out a slender book covered in cement dust, all Harold can make out is a picture of a young girl, a pig, and a spider. Using the last of his strength, Ernest puts the book in Harold's hands. "For Lottie, Charlotte's Web was her favorite story. Promise me you'll take care of her, promise that..." his last breath ends in foaming blood, and his coal-stained hand slips off his daughter's gift and onto the ground.

"Ernest..." Harold whispers, loose rock from the cave-in collects around Ernest as if the ancient library seeks to cradle him in a final embrace. Turning to the two guards behind him, Harold says; "Please help, he may not be dead, we need to get him outside into the light." Though eyes swollen with tears, Harold makes out the blurry gestures of the two guards raising their riot guns at him and the slide and click of rounds being chambered.

Rage at the unfairness of it all, how those in power toss away gifted people once used up, fills Harold until his blood pounds in his ears and the thin veneer of civilization on his soul shatters.

A wordless growl explodes from Harold as he lunges at the nearest guard, he connects at the same time as a sharp "boom" reverberates through the remains of the library and Harold feels warm liquid run down his left shoulder.

Off balance, the guard stumbles backward into his cohort, forcing them both into the corridor of mirrored glass. The still-smoking riot gun flies out of his hand and the wooden butt strikes the concrete floor. The second barrel goes off, the effect is immediate and devastating.

As Ernest had said earlier, the corridor was a house of cards of stacked and leaning mirrored glass, and that house has fallen.

In a deafening crash, louder than the report of the riot gun, the haphazard corridor of glass shifts sideways, not unlike slabs of ice sliding off a steep-pitched roof, the effect is instant and messy as the two guards become a mass of shredded meat in front of Harold.

Ears ringing Harold ambles like a drunkard out of the

collapsed corridor and into the main cavern, the murky light of the Watcher's lamp throwing ghosts of motion against the walls. Seeing the swaying Harold advancing, his body coated in a layer of dust and blood running down his arm, she shrieks, struggles to pull out the large gold anchor from around her neck, and screams out; "Halt, I serve the Lord of the Waves, the judgment and savoir of the righteous, you WILL stand aside."

Here is the woman who has ruined their lives, a symbol of the religion that dominates their daily lives, makes neighbour inform on neighbour, keeps all knowledge to themselves to keep a stranglehold upon their citizens, forcing parents so impoverished that they have to sell their children to save them from starving, children like Lottie, a girl who now has no one. "No, she has me, I made a promise". Harold howls, as he rushes the Watcher, raging clenching his fists until his nails draw blood. Abandoning her attempt at command, she squeals and scurries out of the cavern and into the sunlight with Harold on her heels.

Like a wolf loping after its prey, Harold bursts from the cavern and with teeth bared leaps upon the Watcher, causing them both to go down in a heap on the hard stony ground. A whirlwind of limbs resolves itself with Harold on top of the Watcher and his hands around her neck.

Her face bulges crimson as she breaks nails clawing at Harold's arms, and her heels drumming a maddening tempo upon the ground. His fury spent and back in its cage, Harold realizes that the Watcher stopped struggling long ago. Forcing hands stiffened into claws to release, Harold, stares at the golden anchor around the dead Watchers neck. The symbol and what it represented which kept decent folk like Ernest under its thumb, used fear and intimidation to spread their power and control.

"They won't get Lottie, I made a promise." Harold snarls, as he rips the golden anchor off the body, pushes his battered and bruised body upright, and reenters the cavern.

"You can't go in there, the children are sleeping, I'll summon the Watchers!" A woman's voice shrieks as Harold bursts into the dormitory of the boarding house. His breath fogs out in front of him as he enters the unheated room, the scant moonlight through the iron bars on the windows throws angled shadows against the narrow cots that crowd the room and the tiny huddled forms on them.

"Lottie! It's your Uncle Harold," he calls out.

"I said you can't go in there!" Cries out the matron as she comes chasing after Harold, one arm holding up a lit taper, and the other keeping her thick and warm housecoat pulled tight around her. "Listen here, these are my charges, and..." she stops speaking as the taper illuminates her intruder. Dressed in leathers from hard travel, the man has one arm swathed in bloodstained bandages with a pack over his shoulder and carries a riot gun in the other. As alarming as that is, it's the cold glare and the golden anchor dangling from around his neck that causes the Matron to freeze on the landing.

"My... Lord?" she wheezes, fear bright on her face.

"Leave me now," Harold says, his tone as bitter as the night's air.

Scurrying away, her taper bouncing in her hand, the matron flees back the way she came. When Harold turns back into the room, little Lottie in a thread-bare shift and bare feet stands there peering up at him. "Uncle Harold, What are you doing here? Where's Papa?"

Slipping the pack off his hurt shoulder, Harold kneels down in front of Lottie, her eyes wide with fright. "It's ok Lottie, look what I got you." He opens the pack and removes the ancient doll and the book from the library. Holding the doll out to her, Harold says;"Now you take hold of her and you go gather up your belongings and say goodbye to your friends, we have to leave right away, you're gonna be staying with me for a spell." In the distance, they can hear a bell ring through the night and the sounds of dogs barking getting nearer.

In moments, Lottie breaks from the cluster of unkempt children dressed in tattered clothes, their cheeks hollow with hunger, and puts her few feeble possessions in the pack.

Grimacing, he heaves the pack over his shoulder, and with the hand holding the gun scoops up his feather-light niece until she's clinging to his neck, Harold turns away from the room of children he can't save, holding the only one he can.

"Uncle Harold, where's Papa, I'm scared," Lottie says against his chest, her tears absorbed by his ripped shirt.

"I know you're scared Lottie, me too. But everything will be all right, I promise."

Matthew Daniels

Matthew Daniels has been in every From the Rock book thus far. His story 'Healer's Hoards' appeared in 2016's *Sci-Fi from the Rock*, 'Living and Learning' in 2017's *Fantasy from the Rock*, 'Grow Gold Together' in 2018's *Chillers from the Rock*, 'Eggshell Revolution' in 2019's *Dystopia from the Rock*, 'Rooftop Statistics' in *Flights from the Rock*, and 'Namaily' in 2020's *Pulp Science-Fiction from the Rock*.

In December 2019 he was named a member of the Engen Books Board of Directors.

His first novel, *Diary of Knives*, is set for a November 2020 release.

His flash fiction also appeared in *Kit Sora: The Artobiography* under the title 'Epilogue?'. Daniels has proven himself to be a renaissance man of genre fiction, capable of rising to the occasion of any challenge thrown his way. His short story 'Where With All' was featured in *All Borders are Temporary* by Transnational Arts Production.

As competition over placement in the From the Rock series has improved, so has Daniels steadily grown in his authorial abilities.

He brings with him his science-fiction short stories 'Cloud Storage' and 'Vice and Visibility,' both of which were originally slated to be presented in *Pulp Science-Fiction from the Rock*.

Cloud Storage

Malini floated away from the window of the *Seshat*, their spaceship, overlooking Jupiter. She strapped herself into something like a dentist's chair and connected with the team telepathically. "Are you in the clouds, Quant?"

Quant was already strapped in. His eyes were closed because he was travelling the clouds in astral projection. He spoke Dutch and she Hindi, but telepathy breeched the language barrier. "Just there now. Still can't figure out how long it takes to travel in space. There's nothing to go by. You ever feel like your sense of time isn't what it used to be?"

"Ever since we left," she thought with a chuckle.

Zuma, the ship's launch pilot and another astral projector, sat in the cockpit and watched through cameras. She was mostly resting; her job was to get them there and back. She saw the crew in the psychic operations area – the Lounge, as the team called it in their different languages. She kept tabs on the basics like their orbital position. Jupiter was blocking them from Earth. Weather patterns on the gas giant were the normal levels of cyclonic hellscape, but that wouldn't matter. It's not like Quant's mind could be blown away.

She wasn't party to Malini's telepathic connections because she was working and wasn't involved. The telepath did a great deal of background heavy lifting for the team. After Zuma's experience as a military pilot, she related more to this Indian woman than anyone else in the project – despite her Mexican descent. She turned her attention to a file she had been idly reading in Spanish about the rise in space travel.

It had all started with Dr. Teslin Bisset, a Canadian Astrodynamicist. She also had a talent for astral projection, a kind of extra-sensory perception. Espers – people with ESP – weren't well-known then. She called her brainchild "Infomotion." Zuma got lost in some of the science, and glossed over the descriptions of the equipment itself, but got the basic message: Dr. Bisset had developed machinery receptive to her astral projections that connected to a small nuclear power generation system. "Small" is a somewhat relative term. Instead of the nuclear reaction creating power, it... uh... something, something information. Zuma didn't quite understand what the document meant by "information," because she didn't think of it as something that existed in the world the way energy and matter do.

Dr. Bisset died not long after publishing her work. Her brain simply went dead. But she'd published before embarking on her last ride and the scientific community worked out the safeties for making it so people like Zuma could fly to space without literally losing their minds.

She had to re-read certain paragraphs a few times, and did this leisurely because she was also napping, watching the cameras, and keeping up on her physiological health – important in space. She was an excellent pilot, and her tolerance for long-distance and high-intensity astral projection combined well with her military discipline and training. But she didn't understand how the spaceship reached faster-than-light (FTL) speeds. Infomotion got around the problems of energy-matter relationships that made FTL so difficult, but what did information have to do with speed? She thought about things like high-speed Internet and got confused.

Quant spent hours in the skies of Jupiter, connected telepathically to the other members of the team who were working the run. Or flight. Projection? Anyway, Malini tied him in with Bentley and Cullen. Cullen was a claircognizant, an Esper who gained knowledge that was a little harder to explain. He just *knew*, but had some difficulty with specific influence. He worked best in a team to help fill in blanks. Bentley was a psyographer – someone who could directly imprint the mind into recordings like graphs, pictures, sound images, and so on. Because of him, what Quant saw and heard got recorded in real-time. Cullen's information also went through him and then came out as direct observations no machine could yet reach. Temperature and chemical readings, X-ray, convection patterns, electrical activity, pycnoclines, and even what the liquid surface of Jupiter was shaped like.

Their work was tiring. Five minds working together in a heavily-automated ship. There was no propulsion outside of Zuma's nuclear astral projection setup, and most other functions were hands-off. It allowed the Espers to focus on their efforts. Even with all the time-saving connections their gifts provided them, though, there was so much to cover.

So much.

"Quant?" Malini asked. "Are you in the energy cloud?"

It was another day. Zuma had put their orbit in line

with a nuclear power generator located in an orbital platform above Earth. That was why she'd come out to space. Wasn't it? She shook her head. They'd warned her that the Infomotion drive would give her astral projection a bit of a kick. That must be why she could swear she'd been out in space for a while now.

"Yep," Quant said. "How you feeling, Zuma?"

Zuma's answer was a Spanish pun. Telepathy made it easy for the group to follow. The emotional translation would be "Ugh."

Bentley and Cullen spoke English. Since machine readouts could handle the heavy lifting, Bentley's psyography was concentrated on the nuclear energy's transformations. Like all nuclear generators, the system was using the heat to power steam turbines. That was why their project was so important: nuclear power plants lost most of their energy because all we could do with them was boil water. The team were piggybacking on Quant's astral projection to get a level of direct observation that was possible with ESP but not with technology.

Cullen, though, was the star of the show. "The more we observe," he sent through Malini's thought cloud, "the closer we have to get to any one part." Telepathy could keep thoughts at the same clarity through language, but it couldn't give clarity that didn't already exist in the thought.

Their minds were inside of a nuclear reaction.

"We're getting around the politics on earth by having a reactor in space," Bentley pointed out. "But doesn't our ship…?"

"Please focus." Malini said.

"I don't know how to go any further," Quant said. He missed Holland.

"Malini," Cullen said, "let's get me and Quant in the lead. Quant, try to focus on my sense of what makes the core of the reaction. We can do this."

To Bentley, who was trying to carry the information of their insights into graphs and readings on the ship, the mental zoom-in this required was like that slowing of time and seeping of hyper-active despair that comes with losing one's footing at the top of a staircase. You've got a fraction of a second to appreciate what's about to happen.

Bentley had both more and less mental space than the others while he worked. It was like pushing a stamp into ink and then onto a sheet of paper: you don't generally turn the stamp around to look at it. If you did, it would only be a mirror image anyway, and that gets wonky when your stamp is a psychic metaphor. While he connected the Espers' information with the recording systems, he floated in a kind of grey space, and it gave him more room than the others to think. Not a lot, because he was moving that stamp faster than hands and it weighed more than weight.

But he was confused about their current project. Just for a second. "All right, lots happening," he said. "Let's get on the same page. We're working on the information cloud of the FTL drive, right?"

"Infomotor for Infomotion," Cullen added. "Yeah. Zuma's at the helm. Obviously."

"Could've sworn it was something different for a second there…" Bentley mused.

Quant's job was a little easier. Since Zuma was piloting, all he had to do was bring everyone close enough to look at the connection between Zuma, the infomotor, and (to a lesser degree) the ship's power supply. "Yeah, I get that sometimes," he said. "Not even really sure how long we've been at this now!"

"Something we can think about later," Malini thought. "But right n-"

"What is it?" Bentley almost lost his connection.

"Almost…" it was Cullen.

Malini's surprise either spread through them or equalled their own. It was better not to look at emotions too closely in a psychically shared mental space. "Six!" she declared.

They all came back to their places in the Lounge. Removing their headgear, they followed Cullen, who was propelling himself as fast as he could toward the storage room of the spaceship. He was following a sudden spark of knowledge, like he'd been bounced off his awareness for just a second. His four team mates flooded into the room just as he was opening a coffin-shaped crate in the back and a person came out!

"Konbonwa," the man said. "Kobayashi Oda desu."

Malini touched her temples and squeezed her eyes shut to connect everyone's minds. Zuma was still piloting and they remained in zero-G. Infomotion didn't have things like inertia or G-forces, because the whole point was to get around the problems of acceleration. Quant and Bentley made sure Malini was stable while she concentrated.

"Try that again," she thought to the group.

"I'm Oda Kobayashi," the newcomer responded. "I'm impressed. This is only the second time you've found me."

"Um, try that again," Bentley said aloud. But the mental message got through.

Oda smiled. "I was careless. Terribly sorry. So many

tests. You see, I'm a Chronokinetic."

"I've heard about those!" Quant thought. "Slowing your own perception of time, your body can follow along and you can slip into a kind of suspended animation. That must be why we didn't detect you." He glanced at the rest. "He can change up all kinds of things about how people feel time." Then he refocused. "But why are you here?"

Cullen had wanted to be an action star. That was why he got buff. Oda was no match for his strength, and no amount of change about how he saw time was going to alter his grip.

"Did you know we can alter memory?" Oda answered Quant, unperturbed.

"That's not true," Malini put in. "Even telepaths struggle with that. It's too deep."

"Ah, but what is memory? The mind organizes information by time, yes?" Oda responded.

Everyone experienced a shudder or goosebumps or both.

"All right," Zuma said through the intercom, "We're in orbit around Jupiter. Everyone return to the Lounge with the stowaway. I'll deal with him."

They were all floating their way through. A special garb had been issued for all the Espers, orange and silver, resembling an astronaut suit recoloured and shrunk to a jogging suit. Effectively, a uniform. Technically, the ship had an atmosphere, but protecting people from long-term radiation exposure meant that it was better to stay suited most of the time. The Chronokinetic, like everyone else, was suited up and only distinguishable by his visor.

Cullen kept his grip on Oda as they floated and bounced to their destination, but there was a smaller connection area between the rooms. They had to go single file.

So Cullen, last in line, held on to Oda's ankle. They discussed what to do with the stowaway all the way through to the Lounge, until they stood before the seats they used while concentrating on their ESP.

It seemed to take forever.

Cullen found his mind wandering between arguments and discussion points. There really wasn't that much space between one end of the Lounge and the far end of the storage area. It wasn't a true cargo bay, but more of a locker room. By contrast, the Lounge was a cross between a home theatre and a living room, with the window to Jupiter acting like a film screen.

Cullen released whatever he'd been holding onto in order to set up some straps for a chair. When he stood with the ends of the straps in his hands, turned, and looked around at everyone, he felt a little foolish. It was like walking into a room and forgetting what you came in for.

The main door slid open and closed as Zuma entered from the cockpit.

Bentley said, "Looks like we're all set." Malini had already strapped in and connected everyone.

Quant asked, "What brings you to the Lounge, Zuma?"

Five had been an important number. Zuma looked at everyone in turn. "Just touching base before I rest," she said. She knew she was expecting five. Surely that included herself. No need to be concerned; piloting FTL through astral projection was no easy feat.

The entrance to the tube to storage closed. It did so automatically if left open for more than one minute.

Everyone looked at Cullen, who'd been last in. "Sorry," he said. "Must've forgotten to close it behind me." Then he tilted his chin up at Zuma. "Good work in there.

I see Jupiter is safe and sound."

A round of polite chuckles. He wondered if he was the only one who couldn't quite recall why all of them had come out of storage at once.

"Today's mission is…" Zuma stopped and sighed through her nose. "I clearly need rest. Good luck in the trenches, soldiers." Unlike Cullen, she had no humour, and meant that with a real sisters-in-arms vibe.

Quant accessed a computer terminal built into the wall of the Lounge. He looked up their mission while Bentley prepared the recording devices.

Oda Kobayashi tucked himself away in the crate and returned to his suspended animation trance. Every moment of drawn-out distraction gave him all the time he needed to dislocate the recent-ness of his appearance in their minds. Even if someone had called upon them to think of Oda, they'd have to hearken back as though drudging up memories of kindergarten. He couldn't make them truly forget, but the memory was logged as though it were long ago.

Out of sight, out of…

The team's mission was to observe more about the He3 content and accessibility of Jupiter's atmosphere, after which they returned to Earth's orbit to resume explorations of energy and information technology. Oda took that opportunity, with assistance from Mission Control, to leave the vessel while the Espers were occupied. He swept their memories like footprints in the snow to cover his tracks, then returned to his colleagues at an orbital base.

"Prep a new batch," he told his assistant on arrival. "These ones are picking it up. Make sure we have as much monitoring as possible when we cut their mental feeds; I want to learn from their brain deaths. I have some ideas for refining the process as well."

"Yes, sir," the assistant replied. "Be advised, sir, that we've lost some footage and records of your activities."

He stared hard. "I'll give the operations a review personally before sorting out all the records and documentation. I'm sure you'd recall if anything stood out while I was away...?"

Suddenly the assistant was flat-footed. Kobayashi had been gone for weeks with the last expedition. But no irregularities, such as missing footage, came to mind. "Everything was green, sir."

"Good," he said, and proceeded to the data centre. Couldn't have anyone catching on that he was a Chronokinetic. They might put him in the program.

"You in the clouds, Quant?" Malini thought, with an odd déja vu.

Vice and Visibility

One of the exhaust fans in the town's water treatment plant stood like a sentinel at the turn of a catwalk. It was not an exit for people; it had louvers -- angled metal guards -- on the outside and a mesh shield. Each of its slanted, aerodynamic blades had a slow, ponderous, punctuating swoop. This one glistened with something that looked black in the half-light.

Swoop

A spaceship, shaped like the point of a piton, slit the sky with light and smoke. Dorothy knew that shape was meant for intrusion. There was still a day left to her vacation, and she liked roughing it out in the forest, but had anyone seen the crash this far out of town? She could have been alone but for the screaming of the animals. A heated rush made the trees flap like helpless wings.

Cursing, she set out for what would probably be an early return trip.

Swoop

Mr. Charles was early. More than any of the other teachers, he liked to arrive well in advance because he had a commute. More than that, it gave him time and privacy to indulge in a magazine about cars, or to think through and read about investments and savings.

7:56am.

"Gosh!" He tucked his materials into a corner of the break room and hustled to the classroom's eight o'clock start. He forgot his coffee. A class of boys sat before him.

Swoop

Laura had been having tea with the ladies and lost track of time. Her son, Manson, was home from cadets before she got there from tea. His gun stood in its case beside him. She bustled into the kitchen, eager to get supper started, but she was worried.

At tea, some of the other women chatted about their children's odd day at school. There'd been a crash on the outskirts of town yesterday, and that already had people on edge. All the men had been extra focused in the last few days, but not with work. Sometimes they'd stare a moment too long at a streetlight, or pay the radio rapt attention even when the program wasn't for them. Boys listened to news, commentary on the economy, audioplays they clearly couldn't follow. Men listened even to specials meant for women. And the women's daughters had complained about how all the guys — even teachers and store clerks — seemed to be ignoring them.

"Dad? You hear the door?" Manson called.

Odd. He'd looked right at her as she passed by the living room, or she thought he had. Maybe it was the TV. They were in a suburb, and TVs were all the rage.

"Isn't your mother home?" John answered.

"Yeah," Laura called out. "I'm just getting supper going. Stir fry okay?" The chicken in the fridge was fresh and she wanted to take advantage of that.

No answer.

"Typical," she muttered.

Swoop

Alice was running. Her makeup was blood, grit, tears, and sweat. Police were firing at her. "I didn't do anything!" she screamed desperately, and to no avail.

She didn't understand why none of them were hitting her. It had been dry lately, and it looked like they were shooting at the dust she kicked up while she ran. Mr. Gacy, a friend of Dorothy's, was the best shot in the county. Violence peppered and tufted the street around her. One arm burned with its graze.

"HELP ME!" she shrieked. Women started pouring out of doorways, windows, and street corners. The men were more intent on avoiding the police. Shouts and confusion broke out while some of the women chastised the men. Alice narrowly avoided a fence slat cast off by another shot.

She rounded a corner and struggled to catch her breath. Then she saw something that made no sense: a couple in an odd wrestling match at their front step. He'd been trying to go inside. Now he was weirdly acting like she wasn't there. She gripped and babbled things like "Shame on you!" and "Stop them cops! That's Alice, you ninny!"

He responded by shouting desperately at the police. "Somethin's got me!"

"Didn't think it could be that fast!" It was Mr. Gacy. Instead of looking for Alice around the corner of the building, he led the police in the direction of the struggling couple. Alice noticed that some of the officers were casting searching glances in her general direction.

Women and girls collected either with Alice or near the struggling couple. Some of them called the husband's name, many shouted at the cops, some were calling back and forth between the two groups. The men only seemed to be paying attention to each other.

Swoop

Dorothy had found the alien ship. It had taken a black constellation of flak and there was fire. No good for the dry forest, but she had more pressing concerns now. Iridescent, wounded aliens were still struggling out of the wreck, and they told her knives what she needed to know.

She headed for the car she'd left at the forest's edge, hastily cleaned knives and a hunting bow at the ready. She was still hours out of town, and the military showed up just as she'd been leaving the vessel. Only then did she truly believe what the aliens had told her. Soldiers locked the place down practically on her heels, but didn't notice her.

She forced herself to jog. It was an hour's good hiking to get to the car, and she couldn't afford a stitch, slip, or fall.

As soon as she was behind the wheel, she turned on the radio and gunned the engine. How long ago had the alien effect hit the town?

The love of her life was there, and in grave danger.

It was six hours to town at a leisurely drive.

Swoop

"Hey, sweetie," Laura said to Diana as she came in. "How was sch-" she started, eager to talk about what she'd heard during tea time.

There were tears in her eyes as Diana interrupted her mother. "Jeffrey didn't even notice me!" The door closed behind her.

"Who's there?" Manson called out.

Laura was still working on the meal, the pan ready to go and the rice and veggies portioned out. She was slicing the chicken as she said, "Oh, sweetie. I'm sorry. Why don't y-"

"That wasn't you?" Wayne called from the door to the garage.

Diana was past the gap in the wall that led to the living room. Her beating heart was still facing her mother. She saw Laura's flash of annoyance at being cut off by her dad. Di started, "It was just after Mr. Char-"

Manson had stepped with swift firmness into the hallway behind his little sister, and he was facing the door as he interrupted Di with "Hello?"

Laura and Diana looked at each other, befuddled. Then Manson turned, looking across the empty hallway to the kitchen. A knife floated in the air. He felt the blood that Laura saw draining from his face. Then he rushed back into the living room shouting, "Dad! Watch your six!"

"Dear?" Laura called. "What's gotten int-"

He re-emerged with his cadet's gun and aimed it in her direction, but his eyes were darting a search. "Hands off our dinner!"

Laura was offended. "Now you listen here," and she waved and pointed the knife for emphasis. "I will not-"

Swoop

Mr. Charles had walked home after an odd day. He carried his jacket over one arm and set it down with his hat when he got through the door. Before fixing himself some grub, he turned on the radio.

"That's right, folks. You heard it here first. All the poor women and girls in that town have disappeared!"

A gunshot rang out. He jumped to the window. "What in Sam Hill...?"

At first, there was nothing to see. Then the front door of a house swung wide. There wasn't much wind today, and it was going the wrong direction anyway. The only way that door could move the way it did was if someone had burst through it. He recognized the house, though. It was a fair-sized suburb, but not so big that most people wouldn't know each other.

The house belonged to his friend John from the Classic Car Fan Club.

Diana was running across the street, screaming at Mr. Charles, the first person she saw. "HELP US! MOM'S SHOT!" He stood there, in his window, watching the house with curiosity. Even as she swung both hands and kept crying out, he just turned back to his business.

A car was coming up the road.

The driver glanced at the random swinging of a front door but kept his attention on the road. His brakes screeched his surprise when the bonnet and the windshield made two quick bumps.

The driver's side door made one hefty metallic whump when it opened, he surveyed his Chrysler Fury, and the door whumped closed as he got back in. He continued about his day, wondering where his secretary had gotten off to.

Swoop

Alice watched the couple continue to struggle. The wife was having a conniption, demanding (among other things) that her husband get his head on straight and do good by Alice.

"It looks like it's in front of 'em, Cap'n," one of the officers said.

The captain responded with a meaningful look.

Gacy promptly shot the wife.

Not in the head, or for the heart, even though those were the obvious targets. It was like he was shooting blind.

Alice and most of the other women were pacified from shock and stood there, despite the fact that they were still in danger.

The husband pulled back with relief.

"Apologies for alarming you, sir," Mr. Gacy said while two junior officers felt about on the ground for the body. "We've been investigating ever since that heroic boy shot the first of the aliens in his house yesterday. The military has confirmed that they shot down a ship over yonder." The officer pointed in the direction of the white-grey plumes of fire-battle coming from hours away. "They're gonna lock down the town. They didn't want any announcements because they were afraid the aliens would overhear and we had to be sure people were safe. We were hoping not to start a panic."

The billowing clusters of dresses starting sounding off at once. "What's that gotta do with shooting an innocent lady!" one of them demanded, louder than the others. She yanked open a mailbox and brandished the evening edition at them.

The men's eyes instantly darted at the box, three police opening fire. As dust rose underfoot, yard shrubbery crouched or leaned, and other signs of movement came from several women, the situation went from bad to worse.

Swoop

As car radio announcements and distant gunfire rang in her ears, Dorothy's panic ballooned. By the time she made it to the town, the nightmare was in full swing. She strove to collect the women without the men noticing.

Hungry girls, too terrified to go home, tried to steal from corner stores only to be discovered as floating goods. Some women fought back, out of fear and survival, which only encouraged the slowly rallying forces of military and police. She was told that Alice had gathered people to make for the water treatment plant in the nearby hills.

The night passed. As quarantine snowed over the town, more women got shot as aliens. Finally Dorothy's news about the aliens got passed around.

"They put special radiation in the lights and radios," she said. "Something about brainwave wavelengths? Anyway," she continued, gesturing to different women for supplies, plans, contacts, and tasks, "Some kind of scrambling to guys' brains, so they can't see or hear us. It's supposed to wear off today."

All the women had to do was get somewhere safe and wait.

Swoop

"What do the aliens want with our women?" Gacy asked.

Private Dahmer kept his eyes on a radar screen attached to his gun. That's how they were tracking the invisible aliens. "Got no clue, but they'll pay," he said.

Swoop

Several of the women had gotten hurt trying to get into the ducting; it doesn't work like in the movies. Alice cried out in despair as another of them fell to gunfire. Just her and Elizabeth now. She could hear a fan ahead, and there was only one turn after the catwalk stair.

Swoop

Once the townswomen were as safe as she could make them, Dorothy had used a brook to narrowly get ahead of the lockdown. Now she gritted her teeth with every gunshot as she rushed through the vents.

Swoop

Mr. Gacy and Private Dahmer were side-by-side.

"Town and perimeter secure," came an update from Gacy's radio. They followed Dahmer's gun. There was a fan ahead.

Swoop

Alice and Elizabeth stood with the fan behind them, tears more in their chests than their eyes. The soldier and policeman rounded the corner and stopped, stupefied.

The military comms on Private Dahmer coughed up screams, gunfire, shouts, and other noises of blood and smoke. But the command came through. "They've started appearing as humans! Shoot to kill!"

The pair of men looked at each other. These women looked unarmed. Private Dahmer, under orders, fired at the other woman. She fell backwards into the guard mesh of the fan.

Then both men dropped, an arrow in the back of each neck, and Dorothy emerged out of all hope.

She kissed Alice, fierce and wild.

Swoop

An industrial fan used to help control heat and air quality in the water treatment plant. Its blades hung ponderous and still. They dripped.

Jon Dobbin

A native to the St. John's metro region, Dobbin tied for first place in the 2017 48-Hour Writing Marathon. He describes himself as "the father of three, the husband to an amazing wife, an educator, and a tattoo and beard enthusiast."

He has been featured in both *Chillers from the Rock*, *Dystopia from the Rock*, and *Pulp Science-Fiction from the Rock* before this.

His first novel, *The Starving*, was released in May 2019 from Engen Books. His second novel, *The Broken Spire*, is set for a December 2020 release.

He brings with him two new chilling tales: 'Grace in the Wind' and 'Wings of the Visitor,' the latter of which expands the continuing adventures of Bill Weston, the weird west protagonist of *The Starving*.

Both tales were originally slated to appear in *Flights from the Rock*.

Grace in the Wind

1.

"My sister didn't run away, Mr. Webb. She floated away. Just flew away into the night sky."

Webb leaned over his old desk, picking apart his blueberry muffin with his thick fingers and looking at the young woman who sat before him. It was a good, solid desk that had been passed down on his father's side for who knows how long. Webb would be the last recipient of that honour though. He'd be the last to smooth papers over the scratched and etched surface, to stain it with coffee and tea rings, to wrangle a computer on its uneven bumps and bends. Whoever got it next would probably use it for firewood.

"February is a hell of a time to take flight," Webb said behind a mouthful of dry muffin.

Ms. Mallory Rees sighed, her slender shoulders drooping slightly. Webb pegged her at maybe twenty-five. She was a pretty girl with curly, unnaturally red hair that was piled high on her head. Her pale skin was peppered with freckles and her blue eyes were electric.

"I've heard all the jokes before, Mr Webb. When I told my parents, the police, my therapist, and even my pastor, no one believed me. When the kids at school taunted me."

She brought her steel coloured eyes up to met Webb's own, "Despite all the jokes, all the accusations, I know that Grace would have never left me alone. Never."

"Uh huh," Webb choked down the last of his muffin, and reached for a sip of coffee. "So, you've said that you've talked to the police. Why come to me?" Webb held his cup of coffee in front of him now, letting the warmth rise from the tiny window he'd opened in the plastic cover, inhaling its scent. Coffee wasn't just about drinking, it was about experiencing. An experience in waking up.

"It's a cold case now. No one has found anything new, or even tried to do anything in maybe ten years. My parents aren't getting any younger and it's weighing on them, you know?" Webb did. "It's been over twenty years Mr. Webb. We all just want to know what happened to my sister." Mallory sighed and resettled herself in her chair.

"It's Eddie, please," Webb said taking another sip of his coffee. "That all sounds very hard Ms. Rees, but it still begs the question: why come to me?" Webb was painfully aware that he wasn't a well-known or proven commodity. Private Investigators in the twenty-first century weren't as affordable as Google, and this generation's constant connectivity left people easy to find, even in some dire circumstances. Unfortunately, Webb wasn't making it any easier on himself. He was far from tech savvy, and that left him on the outs of the real go-getters of his profession. Facebook pages, online chat rooms, Twitter – they were all lost on him. His niece, Becca, helped him make some the flyers, but those were a strictly cut and paste job (the real thing, not the computer thing). They depressed him more than anything, as he watched them fade away or get pasted over with the latest band posters. How was anyone supposed to notice them - notice him. There was a time when he would have had an ad in the paper, when he wouldn't be alone in his cold office, and his secretary Karen would field his calls. Those days were long gone. He had one hit case, one that really broke ground and got his name out there, but that was nearly fifteen years ago. Becca sometimes called him a one case wonder. Smart kid.

Mallory squirmed in her seat for a moment, her back arching against the chair, like she had an itch she couldn't quite reach. "Well, Mr - er - Eddie, my family had heard about what you did for the Turnbull family in New York." Eddie nodded along. One case wonder. "That didn't happen so long after Grace had first gone missing. I had heard mom and dad arguing over if they should hire you or not. My dad had kept the news article of what you did in his study." She turned her eyes from him, a heavy shade of purple coating their lids, "he'd bring it out whenever someone brought up Grace." She rearranged her hair, running her thin fingers through the curls before binding it to the top of her head once more. Webb thought he may have seen a tattoo peek out from under one of her sleeves. "Really, Eddie, and I don't mean this as an insult, you're the cheapest on the market. I can't afford much."

Eddie nodded again. He couldn't offer the same things that other investigators could. But what he could offer was a quiet, professional, and discreet service with his large lens camera, and pocket tape recorder. Tools of the trade for any P.I. worth his salt, and essentials when working on his bread and butter - adultery cases. They usually paid decent enough, but even they'd slowed for Webb lately. He played with the idea of retirement more than once, maybe set out to write something, but then one more case came around that looked too good to pass up.

This wasn't one of those cases.

Webb leaned back and sighed. He could feel the extra weight he'd put on, sighed some more. "Alright Ms. Rees, what are you hoping I find?" He said. No use giving anyone false hope. He liked to play it straight, that way no one walked away feeling guilty. "I'm no miracle worker." He could see the young woman sit up straighter, her eyes widened and a smile touched the corner of her lips. He held up his hand. "Get this straight, Ms. Rees, I'm in the discount bin for now, but my pay is by the day. I'll poke around here and there, try to find something new, but I can't promise anything. That means my bill will be there whether you like the news or not." He swivelled his chair around and dug out a sheet of paper from his filing cabinet and handed it to her.

"This is a basic contract. I'll need that before I start. Plus, I'll need your contact info, please write that on there as well. The back is fine." Webb fished out a pen and slid it across to her.

She had the paper filled out in five minutes and he walked her to the door. "Thank you Mr. Webb. This means so much."

"I'll keep you in the loop, but you have my number if you're curious about how things are shaking out."

She started to walk out of the office and down the hall when Webb called after her, "what does your old man think of you coming to see me now?"

Mallory's face sank, a mixture of pity and guilt, "my father threw out your article years ago. We don't speak much of Grace anymore." Eddie nodded, a twitch at the corners of his mouth. He waved and closed his office door. A case was a case.

2

Everyone private investigator had a process. Each case had three pieces to investigate: the history, the people, and the client. Webb knew a handful of people in his field and each had a different process for approaching these things, which order they had to be done.

Webb was a man of particular habits. Traditions really. Three square coffees a day, the same route to work, even the same bedtime routine. Everything had a process. Starting a case was no different.

For a case like this, an older case, logic would dictate that Webb needed to look into the history first; to do his research. Research, however, called for coffee, and there was only one place Webb could get strong enough coffee for this kind of research. Webb wrapped himself up in his old pea coat, scarf covering his mouth and neck, grey toque hanging off his head, and braved the snow.

The thirteenth precinct wasn't the closest to his office, but it was the most familiar. People knew him there. Well, they did at one time. It seemed like every year there was less people to shoot the shit with. A few years back and he could've waltzed on through the building and never get stopped, never be questioned. That was back when you could smoke inside; the good ole days. Now he had to sit and wait with the rest of the schmucks looking for an audience with a detective, or anyone for that matter.

"Mr. Webb?" The receptionist called from behind a thick, plexiglass window, her voice garbled by a speaker that droned a robot voice into the waiting room. Webb ambled toward the door, his coat and scarf hung around his forearm. On approach he nodded and smiled, yes I'm

Mr. Webb, yes you should buzz me in.

Buzz-click and the door unlocked, Webb pushed through.

"Detective Gibson will see you now," the receptionist, Sue according to her desk wedge, pointed down the hall. She was new. Young and bright, she hadn't yet been dragged into the dark, sad underbelly of nine to five work. Especially in this kind of place. Dregs of the earth hung out here, were dragged through here. That weighs on the soul. Beats it down, shows it who's boss. But she wasn't there yet. Lucky her. "He's in his office, third door on the right."

"Thanks Sue."

Marty Gibson was a rusty old screw who was hard on the eyes in his younger years, now his wrinkled and sagging jowls left you with a picture of an old bulldog. There was something about those wet blue eyes of his though, something that brought an eager smile to your face, a readiness to laugh.

"Eddie, you son of a whore," Marty crawled around his desk, his white button up, rolled at the sleeves and open at the collar. "What brings you down to this hole?" They shook hands, both of them shaking in places they didn't have a few years ago. Webb liked Marty, always had, but they were never close.

"Martin, my friend, how's it hanging?" He said, lowering himself into an elderly chair that creaked in regret.

"Soon goin' to retire. What do you think about that?" Marty had returned behind his desk and began to tidy some papers, trying to hide a self-satisfied grin and doing a piss poor job of it.

"You, retired? You mean fired right?"

"Probably be cheaper on 'em," a wheezy laugh bubbled out of Marty's chest, "still time yet." He winked at Webb and squeezed his wrist across the desk.

"Got any coffee around here Marty? I'm parched. They remove that water fountain in the lobby?"

"Yeah Ed, yeah. Let me go grab ya some. Sugar?"

"And cream."

Marty was a stand-up guy and a good detective. They'd met in the army, were stationed together in the Gulf War, and then followed each other into the police academy. They were both just pups. Marty was cut out for it, Webb wasn't.

"So, what can I do for you Ed," Marty said after their usual chit chat, "I know you didn't stumble all the way down here just to shoot the shit."

"Never do Martin, I come for the coffee," Webb tipped his styrofoam cup to him and chuckled. "I got a case. You believe that?"

"Miracles never cease," Marty sipped his own coffee, his smile faltered a little, his eyes narrowed.

"Nothing serious Mart, nothing crazy. Girl wants me to check in on an old missing person's case. Wants me to see if I can't find anything that might have been over-looked." Webb tried to sound nonchalant. Marty was a good guy, but he was also a cop. He wouldn't take kindly to being told Webb was there to do what cops couldn't.

"Is that right?" Marty put down his cup, picked up a pen. "You got a name?"

"Yeah, Grace Rees. Disappeared in '97 while she was supposed to be watching her kid sister. That's all I got. I'm gonna need some more."

"Rees, eh?" Marty scribbled some notes down on a small pad of paper, ripped off the sheet and put it in his pocket. "I'll see what I can dig up. May be some time though Ed, it's an old case and all."

"I hear ya Martin. Anything you could do would be appreciated." Webb stood and wrapped his coat around him and headed for the door. Marty cut him off.

"It's good to see you Ed. Let's grab a drink sometime, hey?" He shook Webb's hand, gripped his shoulder.

"Yeah Martin. Let's do that. You got my number right?" Marty nodded his head, smiled. "Thanks for the coffee Marty, it was swell." He tossed the styrofoam cup into a small garbage can by the door and then headed back into the maze of precinct thirteen.

The office was dark when Webb stepped inside. He shook his collar to clear off some of the snow and hung it next to the door. He thought about checking in with Mallory, but that'd be moving ahead of his schedule, he still wasn't too clear on the history and needed to get his head around it. He kicked off his wet boots and strolled across the office in his socks, not worried about clients this time of day. He sat down in his worn office chair, letting the swivel spin him around as he shook the computer mouse and brought a galaxy of stars flying towards the screen to a sudden stop. The background flickered and changed, a picture of Becca and her dog, Bruno, smiling out at him. Great kid. His brother did good with that one.

He slid the mouse across the screen, clicked on the Google icon, and typed in Grace Rees. The normal things popped up: her obituary, newspaper articles, some tribute pages family or friends had made up. Webb knew he wasn't going to find much substantial on this side of things, he just wasn't familiar enough with it, but he figured he'd get the basics, Marty would get him the nitty and the gritty.

The news articles seemed the best route to take, so he clicked on a few of those, read through them. Their stories matched up, which was a good thing, but there wasn't much of a surprise. Young girl goes missing, leaves her little sister behind all by herself, in the forest no less. The early articles pointed to a fear of wrongdoing, told the tale of the massive volunteer effort to scour the wooded areas, and printed pleas from the mourning parents. Then there was a dramatic shift in approach, maybe it was lack of leads, or maybe something turned up, but the wording the papers used changed. Abducted transitioned to Lost in the Woods which then morphed to Ran Away. It was all fairly smooth. The forest searches slowed down and then she was gone. A ghost. Mallory wasn't in any of the articles except when the "little sister" was mentioned. Nothing more. No pictures, no quotes, nothing.

She showed up in a ten year anniversary article though. It was the high school paper and there was Mallory: fifteen, full of piss and vinegar. Her hair was cut short, bangs sliding to the right to cover her eyes. Her pale lips were a thin line of what? Anger, sadness, resentment? The picture was all business. Still no mention of the floating though. The buzz word was abducted or missing, no strange 'E.T. phone home' or 'I want to believe' back story. It was just a girl pissed about her lost sister. At fifteen social standing and peer relationships were probably held in higher repute than telling your whole story, Webb mused. Then again, Mallory could have lost her marbles in the eleven years since.

Webb switched off his computer and spun his chair towards the window. It was the early dark of winter, snow sliding past the hazy lights of street lamps and the ugly

LEDs of passing cars. January in the city was a mess of weather, impatient people, and poor municipal planning. He looked across the room at the small sofa he purchased for waiting clients and thought about spending the night to avoid venturing out in the snow again. It wouldn't have been the first night Webb spent at the office, those times often revolved about booze or a fight with his ex-wife. Either way, the idea was appealing.

He took a small bottle of whiskey from the drawer of his desk, poured it into a coffee mug, and sipped it. It was a good day. It felt good to get back on the horse and take it for a spin around familiar blocks. The coming days might prove more challenging, but he sipped his drink in honour of a day's work well done. It was the small things, his father had once said to him. Cherish the small things, they make the bad things easier. "Here's to ya dad," Webb said and raised his mug to the window and the falling snow.

3.

The couch hadn't been as comfortable as he'd remembered, and his back was paying for it. He stretched and let all the cracks flow down his spine, a yawn tearing out of his mouth. Webb washed his mouth out with the sip of whiskey he'd left in the bottle and began to scrounge up some coffee.

The history of the case was as covered as it was going to get until Marty turned something up. While he was waiting on that he might as well get started on talking to the people involved. He pulled out pad of paper, a small thing he got in the mail as an advertising gimmick for a local mechanic, and began to write down the people he thought he needed to talk to: the parents, friends (boyfriend?), reporter. It was a start. The parents were the big fish of course. They would fill in a lot of blanks and maybe point him in the direction of other people worth talking to. They'd probably confirm if there was a boyfriend as well.

Webb pulled Mallory's contract and turned it to the back side. He started to dial her number and then stopped. He didn't want to go to Mallory about this kind of stuff too early. He wanted to find out a little more about her first. He sighed, but he needed a way to see the parents. With a shake of his head he dialled her number.

"We still just can't get over the injustice of it. She'd be with us still, she'd have a job and a family. We might even have grandchildren. It's been so hard." Mrs. Rees' weepy voice cracked the refined and proper setting, echoed off its walls and made it somewhat less.

It hadn't taken long for Mallory to arrange a meeting with her parents, and Webb was on his way upstate before the afternoon. By all accounts Bill and Mary Rees were fine people. Bill was a CEO or CFO of some small company, Mary made her living by throwing Tupperware parties and selling make-up on the side. Between the two of them they had a pretty swanky set up. Mary was broken up about Grace. Her face had fallen at the mention of her name, before any of Webb's questions had even begun. Bill was another story; he was all business. Webb could tell he was used to being interviewed, and that he had built up a good poker face during one too many business meetings. Bill stared at Webb like he was on the opposite side of some financial merger, looked at him like he was the enemy.

"I can't even begin to imagine your suffering, Mr. and

Mrs. Rees. I'd like to thank you for taking the time to speak to me about all of this, I know it hasn't been easy. I only have a few more questions." Mary nodded slowly, wiping at her eyes with a handkerchief, her husband merely stared at Webb, daring him to speak.

"What do you believe happened to Grace?"

"She ran away." Mr. Rees spoke for the first time since he shook Webb's hand at hello. His wife cringed at his side.

"I know that there were a lot of theories that were going around," Webb said, "according to the papers it was considered an abduction before the final 'she ran away' theory came to be. Just wanted to know what you both thought about that."

"The papers, the reporters, like to sensationalize things Mr. Webb, I'm sure you are aware of that. It helps them sell. Grace ran away, plain and simple." Webb could see Bill Rees squeezing his wife's shoulder, his eyes never wavering from Webb's own. Mrs. Rees was on the brink of crying once again.

"Okay. My last question," Webb stared back at Bill Rees, forcing himself to appear nonchalant, maybe even a little uninterested. "What do you think of your daughter, Mallory's, recollections of that night?"

A redness started to creep up Mr. Rees' neck, past his collar and crawling over the edge of his jaw line. Webb could see his teeth grinding, his jaw working, thinking up what to say next. "What do you mean?" Mrs. Rees said.

"That Grace just floated away while she watched."

"Our daughter was five years old at the time. She had been disoriented by sleep, or lack thereof, and was afraid because her older sister had dragged her away from her bed and left her in the middle of nowhere. She was a young girl put in a bad situation and her mind responded by making something up. Something that wasn't so terrible." Mr. Rees had bent forward, his elbows resting on his knees. His face glowed red, and veins protruded from his neck and forehead. Mrs. Rees had cringed away from him.

"That's not what Mallory believes," Webb stood and closed his notebook. Mr. Rees fumed, and began to sputter something unintelligible, he looked like he wanted to get up and clock Webb. For his part, Webb just walked to the door. He was finishing with his coat when Mrs. Rees came around the corner, flushed and worried.

"Please Mr. Webb, let me apologize for my husband. We have different ways of dealing with our grief."

"No need, Mrs. Rees. You've been through quite a bit as a family. I understand."

"Yes, we have. Still, is there anything else you'd like to know before you leave?"

Webb looked at her and smiled as he wrapped his scarf around his throat. "Actually, I was wondering if you could tell me about Grace's boyfriend at the time of her disappearance."

Scott Murray's house was small, but well kept. There was a chain link fence surrounding its perimeter that was in need of some fixing, but otherwise it seemed perfectly respectable. Of course, the clean white siding seemed dull in comparison to the fresh fallen snow that surrounded it, and that diminished the house in some way. Webb walked up the stone slab walkway and knocked, his knuckles rapping hard on the navy blue door. He drew his scarf down around his neck and saw his breath as it escaped from his nose. There was no answer.

There lights were off, but it was still daylight and that meant very little. He pressed his hands and nose against the small window in the centre of the door and tried to get a good look inside, but it was no use. What little he did see was distorted and really wouldn't tell him much about Scott's whereabouts. He took a look around, Scott's house was on a big stretch of land, his nearest neighbour was a few yards off, and even then they were separated by a tree line and the fence. Webb decided it'd be all right if he had a closer look. The snow wasn't too hard to traverse as he went around the back of the house. He went up to his knees only once, but once was enough. His pants were wet and cold.

The backyard was tidy. A small shed stood back there, no doubt filled with tools and garden implements, maybe a snow blower. There was a partially buried children's swing set just in view of the moderate sized deck that looked to house a covered BBQ with a bungee cord tying it to a deck post. Nothing out of the ordinary. Scott was Mr. Middle Class. Webb took one last look at the shed. He wanted to get in there, get on the inside, but it wasn't wisest to do a B&E in the daylight, even if the neighbours weren't paying attention. Besides, Webb couldn't really explain why he wanted to get in there. Scott seemed like a regular guy, and he hadn't even talked to him yet. If he was a cop he'd say there was no probable cause. Webb made his way back around the house.

"He's not home," Mallory called to him as he exited the gate leading to the front of the house. She was sitting in her car, a modest, beige Toyota Corolla, a smile stretched across her face.

"I could've used you about twenty minutes ago,"

Webb said as he reached her, placing his hand on the door and looking in at her. "Damn, your car is a mess."

She laughed a light and airy laugh that brought a smile to Webb's face. "Well, I practically live out of this thing. What are you going to do?" She wiped her hands over the seat and knocked some garbage to the floor.

"Keeping tabs on me Ms. Rees?" Webb smiled, but it was a serious enough question. He didn't like his clients keeping a close eye to him. It usually led to messy situations and screwed up investigations.

"Well, I just had a nice angry phone call from my father. After he was through yelling at me, mom told me where you might be. You made some impression: my father hates you, and my mother is worried about you."

"I have that effect on people." Webb looked back at Scott's house, "So where is Mr. Murray?"

"He works construction out of town. He has an apartment he rents during the week and comes back here for weekends."

"No family? I saw a swing set back there."

"Did you? I guess that's for his daughter, he splits time with his ex. Why the interest in Scott?"

"Let's grab a coffee and talk it over." Webb walked to his car, welcoming the reprieve from the cool air. He made sure to blast the heat and pulled into the road, Mallory followed.

They sat in the corner booth of a local mom and pop coffee shop that was trying hard to look like a chain might. Webb paid. Mallory's hair fell in a tarnished flame of rust and copper around her pale oval face. Her pale pink lips almost cracked when she smiled, and they made her eyes a startling blue. She stuck her tongue out as she peeled the lid from her coffee and sipped, the steam rising to tickle her nose.

"So, why this cozy little place?" She spoke first, which almost took the wind out of Webb's sails, her smile almost finished the job.

"I wanted to update you on a few things. Tell you a little about my process. Be transparent." Webb swirled his cup before opening it.

"That sounds like a good idea." She sipped her coffee, her eyebrow twitched in a flawless arch. Webb told her what he'd done so far, his visit to the police and the inevitable wait on the file, his meeting with her parents and what he thought was coming next. In truth he didn't know what was going to happen, but he didn't want to tell her that. Some investigations were just in the air like that.

"So, why your interest in Scott?" Mallory had nodded through the rest of his spiel. He couldn't quite tell if she had taken it all in or not, and was encouraged by her focus on what brought them out her to begin with.

"Well, I don't rightly know yet," He said, near cringing at the lameness of the statement, "but I want to cover my bases. Maybe he knows something, maybe he was involved somehow. I won't know for sure until I lock eyes on him."

"No," she was shaking her head now. "No, Scott wasn't involved. I mean, how could he be?"

"Why not?"

"How could he make her float away like that?" Her big blue eyes locked onto his, fear lying in those azure pools. It was his turn to shake his head.

"Listen, Mallory, we don't know that was what happened?" He held up his hands, placating.

Her stare was blank and unnerving. "I know. I know that it happened. I was there remember."

"Mallory, yes, I know. But I have to cover all the possibilities. I told you that you might not like the answers I found."

She was standing now, her coffee cup forgotten, her long canvas purse clutched in claw like fingers and trailing behind her. "Good day, Mr. Webb. Contact me when you have completed the investigation." And she was gone.

The couch had been even less comfortable than the night before. Webb pushed himself to sitting and tried to ignore his gnawing soreness and creaking stiffness. He leaned forward, letting his back slouch and his head droop. His mouth tasted like whiskey flavoured ashes.

He had stopped at a liquor store on his way back to the office the night before, and bought a flask of whiskey to accompany him on his Google searches for Scott Murray. It lead to nothing. There were an endless number of Scott Murrays. Facebook, LinkedIn, Instagram, Twitter. All shades, all sizes, and none located near him that he could tell. It would've helped if he knew a little more about him, but he didn't. Soon his bottle of rye was gone and his eyes were flashing Scott Murrays when he blinked. He decided to turn in.

Webb took the extra time to ease himself into the day. He was done with the easy things, now he had to play the waiting game. For a PI with only one case, that was torture. If he had another he could at least do some leg work for that, but Webb was stuck in his office with his own stench and feelings of regret.

He felt the urge to call Becca. To see how she was doing. Ask her how university was treating her. Maybe she'd ask him to fly up to see her sometime. When was the last time he'd flown anywhere? Must've been fifteen or twenty years now. Argentina, Buenos Aires. A lifetime.

At some point during the morning he'd managed to put together a cup of coffee and had given himself a whore's bath in the bathroom. His clothes were crumpled and in need of a wash, but they were all he had. A white button down, matching undershirt, and black coat with matching pants. He looked at his blue tie and decided to forgo that kind of formal wear today, leaving the top two buttons of his shirt open. His neck unrestricted.

He sat in his office chair, looking down in the city and thinking about retirement. He wasn't an old man, but the life of a PI was wearing him thin in all ways but physically. Marty had talked about it, why couldn't Webb think about it? Of course Marty was on the police payroll, had a retirement plan and package all ready to go for him when he hung up his shield, Webb didn't have that. If he quit, left it all behind he'd have to pick up some part-time job as a cashier somewhere, or, if he was lucky, a security guard watching over some abandoned building. Keeping out kids late at night. Thrilling. It was a hard sell. He'd have to finish this job first, and then weigh his options.

Webb sat there a little while longer, sipping a cool coffee when the phone rang. Marty scrolled across the screen and he hurried to swipe it open, to answer.

"Speak of the devil," Webb said, a smile in his voice.

"And he shall appear. I knew my ears were burning. Hope you were chatting me up with some sexy little thing."

"Nothing so exciting. Just thinking about old times."

"Be careful, a stroll down memory lane usually winds up being longer than you intend."

"That it does Martin, that it does. So, what's up?"

"I got your file," Marty said making Webb picture his lopsided grin.

"That quick? Marty, you sly dog."

"What can I say, they love me around here."

"Lay it on me."

Marty went through the file at a snail's pace, not missing a single pen stroke as he read it out. Most of it Webb had figured out through his Google search or his chats with Mallory and her parents. It was nice to have a professional, police slant on it though. Emotions always skewed things.

"So get this," Marty said after a pause, "the young sister told the detective at the time that her sister just floated away. Like a balloon high into the sky." He snorted.

"Yeah, I heard that part before." Webb didn't want to picture Mallory's wounded expression from the coffee shop, but there it was haunting him. "Martin, one thing I was really wondering about was why it switched so quickly from an abduction case to just another teen runaway?"

"Let me see," Webb could hear Marty rifling through some papers. "Yeah, here it is. Well, the little sis said she flew away so the detective on scene interpreted that to mean dragged away, for whatever reason. Then they found the note and that turned everything around."

"What note?" Webb was on the edge of his chair.

"The 'goodbye mom and dad' note. Investigators found it in her room."

"Shit," Webb said, feeling anger boiling in him. Mallory didn't tell him that much. Neither did her parents for that matter. "Any mention of the girl's boyfriend, Scott Murray?"

"Oh yeah," Marty said another grin in his voice, "we pressed him pretty hard. Seems that he knew about the plan to run away. His fingerprints were found on the letter, some of his writing too."

"And?"

"And nothing. He was cleared of anything and cut loose. Couldn't have made him too popular though." Mallory seemed to like him well enough, jumped right to his defence. Didn't sound like a hurt younger sister to Webb.

"Thanks Martin, anything else?"

"Nah, that covers most of it. You okay Eddie?"

"Yeah I'll be fine. Thanks again Marty. I'll be seeing you."

Under darkness Scott Murray's house didn't look so pleasant or well put together. The siding glowed a phosphorescent white in its loneliness. The windows were dark, no sign of life. It was a ghost haunting this block, ugly and unwanted.

Webb had parked a block away and huffed it back, trying not to be noticed by anyone. He'd dropped into his apartment on the way here for an extra pair of gloves, his ski mask, and a crowbar. His mind was intent on that shed and what was in it.

His footprints were still there from the day before, joined at times by the wayward prints of an off-leash dog. Nothing else was disturbed. Webb tried to follow his own steps, but without much light it was a challenge.

The moonlight made the backyard a mass of shadows, the former swing set an ominous structure that heaved itself into the sky. Webb had pulled down his ski mask, and made tracks towards the shed. This kind of work was best without light anyway.

The door gave way with two heaves, his shoulder pushing it through after the crowbar did its work. Webb felt around the side of the door jamb, groping for a light switch. When he finally felt the familiar shape he sighed a breath of relief and waited for his eyes to adjust to the dull light.

His wet boots squelched upon the worn wooden floor, water and snow tracking footprints behind him. The shed was filled with the usual accoutrement, an old push lawn mower hung to the side between a pickaxe, and a shovel. It was orderly and well maintained and not shed like at all. Webb walked through the small space, swinging his crowbar, and trying to find something that would implicate Scott Murray in Grace Rees' disappearance, or anything for that matter. At the back of the small space was a wall lined with calendar girls, different women in various states of undress staring with sultry abandon at Webb as he passed, their eyes following him in the gloom of the one hanging light. Webb sorted through the drawers of a built-in cabinet set around the lone window of the shed. Screws, nails, bolts, magnets, and assorted pieces of metal or wood. Webb could feel the weight of the crowbar as it moved at the length of his arm, moving faster now.

The crowbar swung out at the window, shattering it. The sound of it, the movement, surprised Webb, his eyes wide. But it felt good, a cascade of relief rolled over him. A smile cracked his face. He let the crowbar slice the air once more, bringing it down on a drawer he had left open. A satisfying crunch resonated in the small shed. Webb's crowbar led him through the rest of the shed like that, destroying the symmetry, killing the stability, flaying the order. It was over in ten minutes, Webb bent at the waist, panting through the small mouth hole of his ski mask. He was wet all over with sweat, and his chest hurt.

"What the hell is going on out there?" A voice from the darkness, not far enough away for Webb's liking. He slung his crowbar in his belt and ran from the shed, the hanging light flailing in his wake. Shadows followed him in the yellow light that escaped the door, he trampled them as pushed himself through the snow and out onto the street, fleeing for his car. He didn't see the source of the voice, nor did he hear anymore warnings, but he ran and ran. His already throbbing chest now aching with each shallow breath. His lungs were fire, his breath smoke.

Webb passed his car twice before remembering where he'd parked it: off to the side, parked on a small street with only one house on it. He had already removed his mask, stuffed it hastily into his coat pocket, but now threw the crowbar into the trunk of his car along with his gloves and coat. He collapsed into the driver's seat. After he caught his breath he drove away.

4.

His system had failed him. It was supposed to be done in a certain order, and though he tried to do it, it hadn't worked. There was nothing new to point out in this case, no new suspects, no new clues. There was nothing that proved his client was right. In fact, everything pointed to the cops doing a pretty bang up job, covering all their bases, and just not getting the result everyone wanted. Webb knew that was all part of it though, life. Most people had a mistaken view that the police would solve all their problems. Those people had watched too many movies or t.v. shows. The bad guy wasn't always caught, the princess wasn't always saved. More often than not, it was quite the opposite. Webb knew all of this. He knew it from the moment Mallory Rees walked into his office and he told her that she may not like what she found. So why did it feel so wrong?

Life. He felt the urge to call Becca and see how school was going. He wanted to ask her how her grades were, was she still popular? Did she need anything - anything from him?

He had driven passed the Rees house several times trying to see if Mallory's beige car was in the driveway, but it wasn't. Giving up on that, he pulled his car into a small gravel parking lot of a close by walking park. This was the place where Grace went missing, he thought. He looked around the lot for any sign of Mallory, but there were only two other cars there and they were filled with youngsters smoking weed, drinking, having sex. Laughing.

The air was cool on his sweat drenched skin, it felt good. What had he done earlier? He thought as he walked into the small wooded area on a narrow path. More importantly, why did he do it? He had all his answers, his problems were solved, but they weren't the answers he had wanted. They weren't the answers *she* had wanted.

It was going to be a cold night. The fallen snow had turned hard and crunched under his feet. It all made sense, it was wrapped up, it was done. No one actually just up and floated away, and only terrified little girls would say that as they witnessed their older sister abandon them. And if that wasn't the case, if Scott had conspired to make his girlfriend disappear, why hadn't anything come of it? Simple, he thought, there was nothing to look into. The fingerprints on the paper were from a late night of studying, or from when she lent him some sheets of paper to take notes. It wasn't his fault she used the same paper to write her goodbye note. To write her finale.

The path led Webb on, twisting gradually in one direction, abruptly in others. It was a pleasant walk. The trees surrounding him were thin and spaced out, and the night sky had free reign over the path. The moon reflected off the snow, and made the path easy to see. Webb followed the narrow boardwalk, letting it lead him through the wooded area. He took different paths as they came, hands in his pockets and a chill setting into his spine. Still, he walked.

The path ended at a small pond, frozen into a white-blue color that didn't look stable enough to step upon. Webb stopped at its edge, his breath coming in puffs of steam as he tried to peer through the frosty veil. Was this where Grace Rees left her younger sister? Here, far enough away from her house and home that she could run and not worry that her sister would be lost for too long. Did she attempt to run across the pond and fall through? Not floating to her doom, but sinking to it. The fact was, Webb did not know. No one did, nor would they. Some mysteries just stayed unsolved, their answers lost in time.

The moon cast a pale light on the pond, and Webb stared up at it. Was this the same moon that shone down on Grace and Mallory that night twenty one years ago; a moon so bright it displayed every crack or fracture in the snow and ice. Perhaps it was. Perhaps Grace stood her, as Webb did now, and found the moon so beautiful she floated to it. It drew her in, promised her light and warmth and comfort. Promised her that she would never be alone. Webb stared into the moon, his stomach light and fluttering. Webb stared at the moon and could feel his feet lifting to their toes. January was a horrible time to fly, he thought.

Wings of the Visitor

Booker's Shoppe was a staple in Still Creek. The store opened to cater to the miners that rolled into California and the Sierra Nevada seeking gold and fortune. Mr. Albert Booker, a slick business man saw his business boom. And it continued to boom. He took to selling food stuffs, mining and farming implements, ammo, dry goods, even the occasional case of dynamite. Booker was as happy as he was well-off. His wife gave him two sons and a daughter, and they were well respected around those parts. Things were good for the Bookers.

Of course, Albert Booker was dead. His famous Shoppe's windows were dark; boarded up from the inside, the doors too. No foot traffic made its way to his door, nor did the store sell anything for the last several days. Food stuffs and supplies lined the shelves untouched and gathering dust. There were jagged edges torn out of the building at every angle, if anyone was able to view it. Bill Weston feared no one could. He leaned into the door, his back aching as it pushed against the boards he had scrounged from around the store. Leaning over his bent knees to stretch his back he stared Mr. Booker in the eyes. Cold, dead eyes that had filmed over and paled. Weston didn't know what happened to the rest of the Booker family.

"Think it's gone?" a small voice whispered to Weston's left. He turned to the boy otherwise known as Samuel Tucker, small of voice and of stature, his round, moonlike face peered from the back room.

"I fear to hope young Tucker," Weston whispered nodding at the boy, trying to avoid his smart, green eyes.

"Hasn't been much racket for a time," the boy said, creeping into the store's main room.

" 'cept for yer yammering, ya daft idiot," came a growl from behind the counter. The boy shot back in behind the door, his green eyes flashing and wet.

"Easy there Dale," Weston put out a placating hand, "boy is curious is all."

Dale Barrow's pockmarked face came into a shaft of moonlight cast through slats of the boarded windows. Teeth bared, he grumbled, "how 'bout y'all keep yer mouths shut. If it's gone we don't want ter bring it back down on us." His face disappeared into the shadows with a grunt.

Weston ran his hand through his brown hair, and shrugged at the boy who giggled some.

"How's your mama doing kid?" Weston ventured, ignoring an agitated shuffle from next to the shop counter.

The boy shrugged and disappeared into the storeroom. Weston nodded to himself, smiling a little. Allison Tucker's long sallow face appeared in her son's stead, her blue black hair hanging loosely from a high bun into her face. Her pale blue eyes were rimmed with purple and yellow-green, and her pursed lips were pink and cracked.

"Mr. Weston? I-is there something wrong?" She said through ragged breaths.

"No ma'am, just wondering how you were doing is

all. Fit as a fiddle I see."

Her mouth curled at the corners, "I'm doing just fine. My son is taking good care of me." The boy poked his head out around his mother's shoulder at her mentioning, a smile in his eyes.

"That boy is saint and a half, ma'am." Weston winked.

The boy and woman slid back into the storeroom and Weston was left alone, a smile on his face.

Allison was shaken out of her doldrums by the husky whine of horses as the carriage came to a stop. She sighed and looked over to the boy who sat next to her, still dozing from the long trip.

"Time to wake up handsome man," she ran her hand through his brown hair and his eyes fluttered open, a smile on his face as he yawned and stretched. Her only child, Samuel, named after his father who died in the war. It was really for him that she chose to move back to Still Creek. She wanted to keep him close to family who could help raise him to a man. The boy placed his head on her shoulder, cuddled into her. Allison Tucker smiled at her boy.

The door opened to their right and a warm washing of sun spilled in. A large, calloused hand extended itself to Allison and helped her out of the carriage. Their driver grabbed Samuel about the waist and lowered him to the ground with a kind, "there you go boyo."

Allison and Samuel waited on the dusty boardwalk for the carriage driver to unload their belongings. Samuel was watching the slow movement of traffic, the horses, cattle, and people who crowded the main fair. She smiled down at her boy, and watched traffic with him.

"Miss, you might as well explore about some. I'll bring your things to the hotel by and by." The driver said in a gruff voice.

Allison nodded and took the boy by the hand. "Well Samuel, what do you think of your new home," she said with a broad, theatrical sweep of her right hand.

Still Creek stood before them, a town hastily put together by miners and their families, people seeking riches with an unwavering lust. Though it had much diminished in the years since the gold rush, many people remained and the popular landmarks still greeted her eyes.

"You and daddy met here?" Samuel said, his nose wrinkled as he looked over the dusty town.

"We did," Allison began to lead them down the boardwalk, "we were young then, your father and I. He came at the tail end of the gold rush, trying to stake his claim and make his fortune. I was living here with your grandma and grandpa, who had set out to do the same thing as your father." Allison coughed through a smile. "Your daddy didn't find a speck of gold, but we found each other, and that's all that mattered to him." Allison cupped her son's chin in her palm. "You were our treasure, sweet boy."

They walked a little ways more, looking in the storefronts, Allison relating memories when they came to her. "Samuel, you have been such a good boy this long trip, let's get you a special treat from my favourite store when I lived here."

Samuel's smile widened.

"You see that building at the end of the boardwalk? That's Mr. Booker's store. You run on down there and take a look inside. I'll be right behind you." Without any more prompting the boy took off towards the store, laughing.

Allison paused, braced herself against a wall, and barked a hard cough into her handkerchief. She drew it away from her face. Blood, dark and rich, spotted the white cloth. Allison sighed, wiped her lips dry and then put the handkerchief away. She followed her son, trying to smile.

Weston awoke with a start, a dream that had already faded from memory left him shaken and confused. His broad back ached and he stood, leaning into the boarded, wooden door to try and relieve the pain. It was only when he was fully erect that he heard the light tapping behind him. Weston froze in place, listening to the tap as it travelled up and down; searching, probing.

A creak sounded before him and his hand went to his pistol, eyes scouring the darkness. Dale was kneeling on the floor, his right hand gripping the counter, his left holding his shotgun. He too froze in place, his wide mouth in a grimace over his large chin. Weston put his index finger to his mouth and turned to face the door. The tapping continued. A clicking noise echoed the tapping, and a sniffing. Maybe a dog, he thought for a moment before he looked over at Albert Booker's corpse. He stepped softly away and drew his pistol in a slow motion that caused no sound apart from a whispered creak of worn leather.

The tapping began to get harder and louder, now grunts followed it and a shrill whining noise that Weston had never heard before. He turned his head and locked eyes with Dale who remained kneeling, his shotgun aimed and ready.

"If we keep quiet," Weston whispered as he bent to Dale's ear, "we might be able to make it to morning. Try our luck on the road." Dale nodded, gray eyes focused on the door.

Weston tried to manage his breathing, keep it slow and regular, but that small act seemed to make it harder for him to maintain his breath. The fear of collapse became very real, but he pushed on, counting his breaths.

The boy crawled out of the storeroom, his body close to the floor, his green eyes wide. Dale tossed a nervous look at the boy, his head flicking between him and the door rapidly, his shotgun wavering. Weston stared at the boy head-on, their eyes meeting this time. Weston made a shushing motion with his mouth, pointed to his ear and then to the door. The boy nodded and huddled into the wall outside the storeroom door.

A rapid succession of thuds brought Weston's attention back to the front of the building. The door bulged with each attack, Weston cocked back the hammer of his revolver.

"Samuel?" Came a soft voice from the storeroom; it was Weston's turn to whip his head from the storeroom to the store entrance. "Samuel Tucker? Sammy?" Allison Tucker's voice grew louder, more frantic. "Samuel Elwood Tucker! You better not be playing with that pig again."

Weston looked at the boy, tears brimming in the child's eyes, and nodded for him to go to his mother. Dale gave him a look of pure annoyance as he left and they both turned back to the source of violence. The thuds had stopped. The tapping, sniffing, whining had stopped. Everything was quiet once again. Weston's stomach sank.

"Samuel my boy! My handsome boy. Come cuddle into your poor mama."

"Okay mama, but please keep it down," the boy whispered.

"Samuel Tucker," Allison yelled, "that is no way to talk to your mother!" A slap could be heard throughout the building followed by a stifled crying. "Always respect your mother!" Allison's voice returned to a conversational level and then she stopped talking altogether. The whimpering of the boy resonated throughout the quiet store.

Weston dropped his hand, eyed the door, and listened for any other noises. The door was no worse for wear anyway, none of the boards had broken or fallen, but the nails were loose and would need to be tended to if they planned to stay any longer. Though he had meant what he said to Dale, he wanted to leave at first light. Put the town and its dead bodies in his dust. If such a thing was possible.

Dale let out a breath of relief and started to adjust his sitting situation when the thudding and screeching and scratching began anew. A squeal came from the storeroom, the boy surprised out of his stupor. Allison made a roar at him to stop his racket but was drowned out in the frantic attempts to get in.

A large blast sounded off to Weston's left, an explosion that made him clutch his ears in fright and pain. Dale had let loose with his double-barrel, and holes penetrated the door. The unnatural whining and grunting got louder and Weston thought he saw an evil-shaped finger and claw wrap around the inside of the newly formed holes.

Dale cursed at his side as he reloaded, and Weston took up his slack firing away at the door hoping to keep the creature at bay.

Bill Weston rode into Still Creek as the sun sank out of the sky. He tucked his revolver beneath his long brown jacket, keeping it out of sight of the townsfolk. Weston had never been to Still Creek, but he had been to other small towns, and found the local law appreciated discretion.

Entering the town he could hear a guitar playing and the drone of some familiar tune. He trotted his horse toward the sound. Breaking around a corner, he came upon a large circle of people surrounding a little well at the centre of the town. Many people were sitting. More were standing on the outskirts of the circle on the boardwalk, leaning into the buildings. At the centre of the circle, closest to the well, were a handful of people leading the song, a small woman played the guitar and she was flanked by a man, a boy, and a girl who sang amiably enough.

Weston guided his horse to a hitching post and left it there to water itself so he could mingle amongst the townsfolk. Few of them noticed the newcomer in their midst, those that did gave him a nod and let him go about his business. The songs changed as he moved around, still an uplifting psalm that reminded Weston of his childhood. He settled in to watch the concert next to a scar faced man who chewed on a hand rolled cigarette.

"Just get in town?" the man growled around his cigarette.

"Yes sir. Didn't quite expect such a lovely welcome for me."

"I hate to disappoint friend, but this is not for you," the man chuckled, "this is, well, this is something." The man trailed off and returned his attention to the entertainers.

Weston lost his attention on the band as they finished up the tune. A hesitant silence fell over the crowd, all of whom kept their eyes on the centre of their ramshackle prayer circle.

"Speech," a rough voice called from the other side of

the crowd.

"Comfort," said another behind Weston and "prayers," coughed a third.

The players in the middle looked around at one another and the elder man stepped forward, adjusting a slim pair of spectacles. He was a tall man, slim by nature, with bony shoulders and long thin arms. His gaunt face was covered in a sparse, blonde beard.

"Speech, Albert, speech," came the first voice again as the man next to Weston tossed down his cigarette and spat.

"Friends, neighbours, we are in an hour of need," the man's voice was rich and pleasant and carried on the wind. "Our town, our home, has been besot by a terrible evil that we have not been able to destroy by man-made weapons or conveniences." There was a mixture of nodding and shaking heads in the crowd, children held to their mother's dress skirts. "Now is not a time for fear, however. No, we shall not be afraid. We must put our faith in the Lord, our God. As Psalms tells us, 'but you, Lord, are a shield around me, my glory, the One who lifts my head high. I lie down and sleep; I wake again, because the Lord sustains me. I will not fear though tens of thousands assail me on either side'."

There was a smattering of cheers and the crowd began to disperse. Weston looked over at the pock faced man, "well that was something. What the hell is going on here?"

The scarred man gave him a cold look and shook his head. "How long you aim to be in town?"

"A day or two."

"Well, don't let it trouble you none. It's the town's problem." He nodded towards a pale woman and her young son, both looking as confused as Weston felt. "Now that's who I pity, right there."

"What do you think it is?" Dale ventured, sitting against the shop counter.

Weston shrugged. They had done their best to board up the holes, reinforce their defences, but more moonlight pushed its way through than before, pinpoints of white light now struck Dale in the chest.

"Nothing I've ever seen before."

"You and me both," Dale leaned forward, "I've lived in this town for near fifteen years, and never did I see that before these past few weeks. You ask me, they brought it up from down south with 'em. Maybe even some sort of godless creature from the people wut was here before."

Weston shook his head. Dale's face became grave, a grimace of malice glazed over him, his eyes blank.

"What the hell do you know? You just got to this town, never had to deal with either of those types before have ya? No sir. Well, heave off, Bill Weston."

Weston matched eyes with Dale, but made no movement other than to keep an eye on Dale's hold on his shotgun. "Easy there Dale. I didn't mean to cause a ruckus, just seems to me that if the another group had something like this in their pocket, you'd think they'd have used it before this."

Dale's eyes relaxed, his grip on his rifle loosened, "well, since you're so smart, what do you think brought it in?"

Weston considered this for a moment. He eased himself to sit a little more upright. "Well sir, this is a mining town is it not? Perhaps our miner friends dug a little too deep looking for gold or silver or coal or whatever it is they dig for around here."

"Our diggers are pretty good, but I don't reckon they could dig a hole to hell." Dale said and leaned back.

Weston smiled and nodded.

A groan came from the storeroom. Dale spit. "What'll we do about them?"

"What d'ya mean?"

"You know what I mean, the woman's dying and the boy is a useless cry-baby. There ain't nought we can do for 'em. If you mean to leave at first light, we best leave them behind."

Silence fell as the men's eyes met.

The boy crawled out of the room again, face pale and eyes dark, "mama needs some water." His shoulders slumped as he rubbed his eyes.

Dale turned his head away from the boy, giving Weston a knowing look as he did. Weston sighed, dug in his pocket and pulled out a small flask. He shook it, heard liquid slosh inside of it and held it out to the boy.

"Here you go kid. Should be enough for your ma in there."

The boy took the flask and edged his way back to the storeroom.

"How's your mama doing anyway?" Weston blurted.

The boy's eyes turned to the floor, and he scuttled into the door from whence he came.

"Not much more can be said about that," Dale yawned and stretched himself out on the floor. Weston watched his silhouette descend, shotgun and all. Only a few hours until daylight, he thought catching sight of Albert Booker once more and his distorted features.

The creature descended on the town the second night after the prayer circle. A thunderous flap of wings cracked overhead followed by a high-pitch screech.

Dale Barrow had volunteered to stand watch at the edge of town that night, himself and Albert Booker had set up on opposite sides of the town. He carried his double-barrelled on his shoulder and sat on an upturned bucket he had borrowed from the saloon. At the sound of the creature's cry, Dale spit out his twisted cigarette and jumped up from his bucket. He ran back into the centre of town.

The streets were already empty, most folks had retreated into their homes once the sun had gone down. As Dale ran through them, his shotgun swaying, he could hear the frantic explosion of boards being hammered in place. He thought of his own wife for a moment, and then focused on the sky.

The newcomer, Weston, was at the well as Dale turned the corner to it. He had his pistols drawn, but he seemed to be confounded.

"What the hell was that?" Weston stammered when he recognized Dale approach him.

"Town business," Dale said through laboured breaths, "why the hell did you leave your lodgings?"

Weston gave him a sly grin. "I was curious."

Dale spit and measured the man before him. Idiot, was the only thing to come to mind.

A scream and gunshots drew their attention, and both men took to their feet towards Booker's store. Dale fell behind the younger Weston, but he saw the creature first. As it took to the skies on its black wings; he fired both barrels and knew he'd wasted his shells. It flew into the blackness of the night, its odd scream hanging on the wind.

He turned his attention back to Weston, who was crouched in front of Booker's. It was only when Dale caught up to him that he noticed the pair of boots pointing their toes to the sky. Booker lay there, shivering and spilling blood. He was slashed from head to toe. His weapon lay by his side, torn asunder.

"Goddamn." Dale said, but did not lean close to the dying man. He kept his eyes above him.

"Is he alright?" A small voice came from the barely opened door of the shop.

Dale and Weston jumped back. Dale pointed his rifle at the small, pale child that stood in front of them. Weston grabbed the barrel and pointed it away from the boy.

"Damn it boy," Dale sighed recovering his gun with a jerk.

"Samuel? Samuel get back in here." Another voice came from within.

"Who do you have in there with you little man?" Weston tried to peer around the boy.

"Who cares. That thing could be back any second." Dale said and grabbed Booker by the collar and dragged him into the store, pushing the boy out of the way.

Weston stood and looked over his shoulder. Clouds passed over the waning moon, and the beat of leather wings echoed over the town. He stepped into Booker's Shoppe and locked the door behind him.

The night had remained quiet. Weston heard the flap of wings from time to time, but they were far off. They heard no more of the creature's cry. Weston peeked out a bullet hole to the empty street, the sky was a deep blue and the stars were disappearing from the sky.

"Dawn's approaching," he said as he turned to Dale.

"Umhmm," Dale was studying a wayward jar that he had found under the counter at his right.

"Think we can make a break for it with sun up?"

Dale laid aside the jar and stared at Weston over arms crossed over his shotgun. "We might do. Where you planning to go?"

"I don't know," Weston said staring at the floor, "is there a safe place to go 'round here?"

"Come sun up even the streets will be safe," Dale said biting his nails, "but most folks take care of their own 'round here. We board up our homes at sunset, stay real quiet, remove boards at daybreak. Simple."

"What about you and him?" Weston said thumb pointing to the body of Albert Booker, "you two were out and about tonight."

Dale nodded, "sure we were. We volunteered to keep an eye out, to help if we could. Not many other people do." He spit out a fingernail.

"Have y'all tried hunting it?"

"Nah. Doesn't leave regular tracks on account of its wings. Though, I 'spose the mine is a good a place as any to check. Problem you'll have there is getting people to go do it. Everyone is scared. No one's been able to harm it, and it keeps killing our friends and neighbours. At this point, we're more like prisoners than anything else."

"What does it want?" Weston said aloud to himself.

Dale shrugged, "blood and death. That's all I can figure."

Silence folded over them. Weston turned his attention back to the bullet hole and what lay beyond it: a silent town, an empty road, and a slow end to the night.

"Samuel," Allison's voice rose from the other room, "you come back here."

Several stomps followed, and the boy lead them on into the front part of the shop. His eyes laid upon Weston and Dale and he hesitated. He shook his mop of dark hair, a signal to himself, and with tears leaking from his green eyes he dashed forward and grabbed the door handle trying to extricate himself. It wouldn't budge.

"Stupid idiot," Dale spat and moved towards him.

Weston moved too, making to grab for the boy.

The boy dodged their hands, Dale made a kick at him that he skirted, and he landed on the door kicking and punching.

"Samuel! You get back here right now," a scream came from the storeroom. The boy pushed forward and a crack erupted from the door.

"Grab him!" Dale pressed forward, dropping his shotgun.

Weston grab the back of the boy's shirt and pulled him back. The boy pulled away his shirt collar tearing off in Weston's hand and the boy disappeared into the twilight hour.

Samuel's mother coughed into a handkerchief, lace surrounded its edges. Samuel liked to rub the lace on his nose and chin, liked the softness. Now the handkerchief was wet and darkening in the middle.

His mother had shown him around the town. He'd seen the tavern where his father spent his free time, the inn where his mother had worked as a girl, and the small house where his maternal grandparents had lived and where his mother had grown up.

They were all dead. The last place they visited was the cemetery to put flowers on their graves. Samuel hadn't minded, he never knew them, but his mother cried.

The store they had visited earlier was fun. He had enjoyed the caramel candies, and the owner who had a large chin whisker, and joked with him, and stuck out his tongue when he laughed.

It was later now and his mother brought him to some sort of gathering where a lot of people were sitting around, talking and singing. Samuel enjoyed the singing, but hoped they would make a fire. A fire right there in the middle of everyone would make everything just right. A big fire that cast shadows and orange light on people's faces, and warmed his hands, and crackled and smoked a sweet smell.

The store owner stood in the middle of everyone and every now and then he would talk about God or the bible.

"Are you okay momma?" Samuel held his mother's hand and looked up at her.

"Of course Samuel. Don't worry about your mother. We'll be just fine." She smiled at him, but her skin was white and her lips red like some of the porcelain figures she had back at their house they lived in with his father. He missed his father.

They walked along the boardwalk after the circle of people went home. Samuel heard banging coming from some of the homes they passed and asked his mother what everyone was doing. She didn't know.

"Momma?"

"Yes sweet boy?"

"I love you."

His mother's smile widened and she kissed him on the forehead, "I love you too precious boy."

"Samuel you're a bad boy! You get back here right now," Allison stumbled out of the storeroom, leaned against the doorframe, her hair loose and hanging in her pale, blood smeared face. Her eyes scanned the room, falling on Weston and Dale in turn; she stifled a cough, closing her mouth and letting the dull wheezes shake her.

"Allie," Weston turned toward her, "Allie, go lay down okay? We'll bring you Samuel."

Allison looked at his hands and saw the light, torn cloth hanging from Weston's hand.

"What'd you do with my boy?" Her voice was low, her eyes bleary but drawn on Weston.

"He ain't done nothing with your idiot child," Dale spat, "brat done run off. Likely breakfast for yonder beast now."

Weston shot Dale a contemptuous look, and held out his hands to the woman whose eyes didn't waver from him.

"Gimme my boy," she growled, blood dripping from her mouth.

"We'll get him Allison," Weston said.

"Like hell we will," Dale shouted, "little Idiot is dead and we both know it. Only a couple of hours left 'til daylight, then I'm going home."

"I'll go get him then." Weston nodded at Allison, turned to the door and tore down the boards.

"Didn't take you for a fool Weston," Dale said picking up his shotgun and taking up his place next to the counter.

Allison wavered in place for a moment and then slid to the floor, hugging her knees. Weston gave her one more look, wrapped the boy's torn collar around his right hand and left the store.

He bent toward the dirt road, still stained with Booker's blood. There were small signs of the boy's passing: a scuff of a shoe, displaced rocks. They lead to the east side of town, toward the hotel and the graveyard. Weston followed them.

The town was quiet, a sober feeling of uncertainty hung in the air. At each building or home he passed, windows were boarded or shuttered. In some of those places Weston had no doubt bloodshot and fearful eyes watched the empty roads.

Weston followed the boy's tracks to the hotel, an average size, well-crafted building made of dark Pepperwood. It was two stories tall and held 10 rooms, each one occupied including one by Weston himself. It was a well run establishment by a local widow named Clarissa St. John, who kept it clear of trouble. The front door of the hotel stood closed, though there were handprints embossed in blood about the middle of it. The boy was not granted entrance. Weston grunted and spat and continued tracking the boy.

A screech broke the silence of the sleeping and fearful community, Weston ducked and looked towards the sky. The sound was far off, but a red light broke through the clouds at a distance, and a steady flap of wings lapped against Weston's ears.

Weston ducked into the graveyard following the trail, in the twilight gloom he could see the boy sitting abreast of two grave markers shaking his head. The screeching had stopped, but the thunderous flapping of wings approached closer and closer. Weston moved toward the boy who turned to him, tears staining his reddened cheeks.

"This is my grandparents," the boy sighed. "I didn't know them. My mama says they were real nice, that they farmed and had their own animals." He looked into Weston's eyes, "even a bunch of pigs. I've never seen pigs before."

"Boy we have to get to cover, we…"

"There's something wrong with mama right?" The boy sniffled and ran a sleeve under his nose. His glistening eyes brimmed over and stifled sobs wracked his child's body. A deep heaving of his lungs and throat that emanated as sighs and grunts.

"Yes, boy, your mama ain't right," Weston said, "she's awful sick."

"I knew it. Yes, I knew." The boy whispered rubbing a fresh bruise growing on the side of his face.

A clap of wings rumbled, Weston stood and grabbed the boy by his shoulder, "we got to get to cover". They moved through the graveyard, a grand space of flat land that bordered the town behind makeshift wooden fences. He looked to the skies but could not see the red glow anymore.

"Where are we going?" The boy tugged at his sleeve.

"Cover. The first we can find." Weston drew his pistol and kept it by his side. They pushed on.

A thud reverberated behind them, a high-pitched grunt accompanied it. Weston froze in his tracks. Heavy breath panted at their backs.

Weston pushed the boy away from him, spun on his heel, "run, boy, back to the store," and fired twice without looking.

Dreadful crunches of bullets impacting flesh assailed his ears, a harsh whine and chittering followed. Weston could not quite comprehend what stood before him, but an image of a bat flashed in his mind. Its long, leather-winged arms wrapped around its massive torso, its rodent face split by a fleshy mass of cartilage, under black eyes devoid of emotion, save for intent, that looked down upon him. Its mouth opened and a blackened tongue lolled out between large sharp teeth, and the red glow began to emanate from its gullet.

Weston fell back, striking his shoulder on a makeshift wooden cross as he did. His mind reeled and his body, driven by some primal instinct to survive, forced itself to crawl backwards away from the creature. Though it pained him, he could not move his eyes from it.

The creature unfurled its wings and displayed its impressive wingspan that blocked the view of the rest of the world from Weston's sight. The wings were as black as pitch, and Weston had the strong feeling that any light that fell on them would just be enveloped and devoured by the utter darkness displayed there. Without his attempt or desire, Weston's eyes focused on a corner of the onyx field held within the creature's wings. As he focused there he began to see stars form in the darkness, bright white lights that spotted the wingspan almost completely. After the stars began to fall and fly and shoot, they formed constellations not like those Weston was used to, and he tried to study them. Uncover their shapes and patterns, but the more he did and more muddled his mind became.

"Mr. Weston," a warbled and muddy shout came to his ears, "get up!"

Weston moved in slow motion, but the small voice began to work on his hypnotic hold. He forced himself to look to the right and saw two holes at the edge of the right wing. Bullet holes. Those holes punctured the galaxy that had bewitched him, he could see the yellow glow of morning through them. The fantasy crumbled down.

Weston fired the remaining four shots into the creature that sent it reeling. Weston made a drunken attempt to stand with the help of wooden crosses, and hastened to reload his gun. His fingers fumbled at the bullets he dragged from his belt. The creature behind him screamed and Weston fell to the ground again.

Red light spewed out of the creature's mouth. It crawled toward Weston snapping its jaws. He fired three more rounds, his hand jostling back with recoil. The thing reared back and howled once more, and Weston got to his feet.

Weston ran to the edge of the graveyard, his gun hand shaking. The monster flapped its wings, shook its massive head, and screamed into the lightening sky. It took off, its leathery winged arms lifting it from the ground, the red light barely visible now. It flew towards the mountains in the distance.

The boy ran to Weston's side and grabbed his free hand. "Let's go, please."

Weston hesitated, watching the beast fly away, but he turned to the boy, "okay. Yeah, let's get you to your mom." Weston took the boy by his hand and they walked toward Booker's Shoppe, looking over his shoulder as they walked.

They were silent as they walked. The sun rose in front of them, a red sphere that leaked purple and orange hues into the sky around it. The creaking sound of nails being removed surrounded them, and pale, round faces began to appear in windows and doors, their eyes holding questions that would never be asked.

When they arrived back at the shop Dale had emerged, some wood and nails lined the boardwalk in front of the store, and he smoked a long cigarette. As they approached, his eyes widened behind a deep inhale, and he nodded to them behind a stream of smoke, "didn't figure you'd make it. And none the worse for wear, it seems."

"I wouldn't say that," Weston growled and prodded the young boys back, "go on boy. Go see to your mother." The boy left his side, but was slow to release his grip of Weston's hand.

"The monster?" Dale took another long drag on his cigarette.

"It made an effort. But, as you say, no worse for wear," Weston made a show of dusting off dust and dirt.

Dale nodded again and leaned into the storefront, a sigh accompanying his next exhale. "Think you killed it?"

"No. I shot it up a bit, saw it bleed, but it was like I just stung it a little."

"But it didn't kill you," Dale whistled through his yellowed teeth, "well ain't you a lucky son of a whore." A thin smile grew around his cigarette.

Weston stared past him and walked into the store.

Samuel's mother was dead. He wasn't surprised when he found her, pale and slumped on the floor. She had specks of blood on her lips and it reminded him of when she'd get dressed up for town dances, and would chase him around their small house threatening to paint his face in her lipstick kisses.

He heaved his shoulders and cried and kissed her hands and face and eyelids. When Weston came into the room he turned and ran to him, wrapping his arms around the man's strong stomach and squeezing. Weston hugged him back. The two never said a word.

A crash broke the boy's hold on Weston. They both turned towards the store entrance. Debris was strewn across it with Dale, bloody and broken, among it.

A groan rose from the pile of broken boards and dust in front of them and Weston drew his revolver, checking to see if it was loaded. The creature's horrible cry broke through the ruined store, screams followed it from outside; the town renewed in its panic.

"Behind me, boy," Weston said guiding Samuel around his side and pointing the gun at the jagged hole that was once the store entrance. The beast's head entered first, it moved in a steady and slow motion, tasting the air. It turned in Weston's direction with its mouth lolled open, the red glow crawling out from within.

Six shots were fired at the creature and it recoiled into the street with renewed quickness, it chittered and growled as it went. Weston reloaded again, and paced around the room, the boy, crouched next to his mother, watched him.

The darkness on Weston's granite face lifted as he moved towards a window at the back of the store and removed the remaining boards. He tossed a table out of his way and stood fast as his eyes caught sight of a small box; a smile grew about his face.

"Get out boy," he said, grabbing the boy by the shoulders and lifting him to his feet. "Jump out this window and run back to the hotel." Samuel looked into his cobalt blue eyes and started to protest, tears stop streaming down his cheek.

"Now, now. No need of that young Tucker. I'll be joining you soon. Tell the matron to have a rye ready for me," with that he forced open the window and lifted the boy to the outside.

"You promise," the boy said, hanging from the edge of the window.

"I do," the man returned and lowered him down. He watched until he ran off and then returned to the box he found. The box labelled T-N-T.

Dale coughed and tasted the iron of his own blood slick on his tongue. He could feel himself moving, but when he attempted it, he couldn't move on his own accord. Yet still, he moved across the wooden floor of Booker's Shoppe.

"Easy there Dale," Weston grunted from behind him and felt another jostling movement. "Won't be long now."

Dale managed to roll his head back so he could look at the man dragging him. He tried to speak and found that he could not do that either, beyond a sickly sounding wheeze. He had hoped to curse.

The beast shambled into the Shoppe, crouched and crawling along on its winged arms and feet. It exuded a pungent odour of the wild and dried blood that caused both Dale and Weston to gag.

"Here's our visitor," Weston exhaled, "a little ahead of schedule, but we'll have to make due."

Weston sat Dale up against the wall under the open window. Dale could feel the cool air climb down his head and shoulders, and it soothed him some.

The creature was cautious. It crawled slowly, and sniffed at everything around it, snapped at some things and dragging others off shelves with its strange arms. Its eyes remained fixed on Weston.

Dale's ears popped and he could see smoke gather in front of him as Weston shot at the beast two more times. A high-pitched whining followed and a growl. The room filled with a red light.

Weston's hands were on him again, and Dale was thrown through the air landing on a patch of dew covered grass in the morning shade. The impact made it hard to breathe, but breathe he did.

A moment later he could feel and hear an impact to his side followed by hands grabbing him again. He was hefted into the air and thrown over a strong shoulder. "I hope this works," he heard Weston mutter as he ran away from the store.

Dale forced his head up, in the rising sun he could just make out the window of Booker's store and the snapping face of the creature as it tried to force its massive frame through. Dale dropped his head, sapped of energy, and allowed himself to be carried.

The explosion tossed Dale and Weston through the air, and they both landed atop of one another, groaning. Booker's Store, a local landmark, was reduced to flaming wreckage with pieces spread throughout the town. Weston and Dale could feel the heat from the fire on their faces before they both collapsed, unconscious.

Weston found the boy amongst the crowd that had gathered in front of the burning building. Some people stood ready with buckets, but none approached. Nothing moved within.

"It's perfect," the boy said as Weston rubbed his aching arm, "it's just right."

Weston nodded and put his good arm around the boy's slim shoulders. They watched the fire burn as the sun rose behind them.

FROM THE ROCK STARS

A COLLECTION OF SHORT STORIES
EDITED BY ELLEN CURTIS & ERIN VANCE

From the Rock collections alternate between three main genres: Science-Fiction, Fantasy, and Chillers. This collection contains the best examples of all three, in roughly equal measure. All stories are kept to a PG-13 standard to be as widely accessible as possible.

Those who read the series regularly will notice that there are some names that show up again and again. These individuals are known as Rockers: authors who have been included in at least three different collections, and who have proven themselves excellent at each of the main three genres we've challenged them with. They are Ali House, Chantal Boudreau, Jeff Slade, Jon Dobbin, Matthew Daniels, Nicole Little, Paul Carberry, Peter J Foote, Sam Bauer, and, Shannon K Green. Collectively known as the best in genre fiction storytelling in Atlantic Canada.

Or, colloquially, as the Rock Stars.